DOUGLAS WYNNE

ILLUSTRATED BY

MAT FITZSIMMONS

Cover artwork by Matt Bright/Inkspiral Design

The verse quoted on page 18 is from
"The Battle of the Lake Regillus" (1842) by Thomas Babbington Macaulay

ISBN 978-1-077266-83-4 (paperback)

First Edition: August 2019

www.dougwynne.com

ALSO BY DOUGLAS WYNNE

The Devil of Echo Lake
Steel Breeze

THE SPECTRA FILES
Red Equinox
Black January
Cthulhu Blues

SMOKE & DAGGER

PROMETHEUS
PRESS

For my dad,

aerospace engineer, scuba diver, daredevil

He would often regard it as merciful that most persons of high intelligence jeer at the inmost mysteries; for, he argued, if superior minds were ever placed in fullest contact with the secrets preserved by ancient and lowly cults, the resultant abnormalities would soon not only wreck the world, but threaten the very integrity of the universe.

–H.P. Lovecraft, *The Horror at Red Hook*

Do you believe then that the sciences would have arisen and grown if the sorcerers, alchemists, astrologers and witches had not been their forerunners?

–Friedrich Nietzsche

Only in the irrational and unknown direction can we come to wisdom again.

–Jack Parsons, letter to Marjorie Cameron 1946

Prologue

Carl Bauman lingered at the window of the pipe shop and regarded the wares through the plate glass. A sign for bomb shelters emblazoned on a brick building across Wiltshire reflected back at him on the afternoon sunlight until a streetcar eclipsed it. Eight hundred dollars for a hole in the ground full of canned beans. Who could afford that? Maybe the Hollywood producers whose cars he serviced—pretentious twits who smoked pipes and wore sport coats. Certainly not him. Anyway, the war was over and Carl was a cigarette man, so what was he doing here, cooling his heels on the sidewalk when he had an appointment three doors down and one flight up? He wiped his hands on his trousers and sighed.

He'd been to the sparse office twice before and had never been nervous until today. Those visits had been easy money. Today was different. He was finally going to meet the enigmatic Mr. Parsons and—his hunch told him—take a drug that was supposed to make him psychic. No one had told him outright that this was the next step of the experiment he'd volunteered for. He'd worked it out by deduction and the knot in his stomach that told him to stick to dry toast and black coffee for breakfast. The funny thing was: Carl had never been one to trust his hunches, which was why he'd progressed this far in the first place.

He heard about the study from a fellow tenant at the boarding house on Bunker Hill, an actor named Ray who'd brought home a flyer he found glued to a telephone pole:

PERSONALITY TEST
CONTRIBUTE TO SCIENCE / EARN 60 CENTS

Carl had brushed it off as a scam until Ray came home with a new fedora and change in his pocket the next day, claiming it had only taken half an hour. Carl made fifty cents an hour at the Gilmore filling station on Fairfax. So what was the catch?

"It's for USC. They just ask you about your dreams and if you ever win at gambling."

Sure enough, Ray was right. But Ray only went the one time and was never called back, while Carl had banked an easy buck-twenty so far, and was back again today for a third test that promised another dollar just to sit in a chair and smell some incense. He didn't think they could be testing poison fumes on humans, like the krauts did during the war, but comparing his survey answers to Ray's had convinced him that the college was studying psychic powers. Ray had a dream one time about his uncle dying right before it happened—and his hunches for auditions and horse races occasionally paid off. Carl, on the other hand, had eternal bum luck and no dreams that he could ever recall.

The paper questionnaire was administered by a pretty, dark-haired receptionist named Salome. The second test, the one he and Ray couldn't compare notes on because Ray wasn't invited to take it, was done by a quiet, swarthy young man in shirtsleeves. Carl couldn't remember the man's name—something Persian sounding—but he did remember him referring to a Mr. Parsons who had a background in chemistry and currently held a position in the Pharmacology Department at the University of Southern California. Carl noted that it was *Mr.* not *Dr.* Parsons and that the tests were being conducted off campus in an empty office space. It felt a little fishy.

The second test was a series of card games: Guessing the symbols on facedown black-and-white cards with stars and circles and squiggly lines and such, then describing the feelings he got from looking at various tarot cards. Again, easy money. He'd left that second session convinced that the people running the experiment were keeping aspects of their work secret from the college for fear of ridicule and maybe getting their funding shut off.

Having demonstrated no psychic talent in the first two sessions, Carl expected the pharmacology part to rear its head today. He'd read the fine print on the consent waiver Salome had him sign at the first session, which included something about sampling various non-toxic fumes. Given that Carl breathed gas fumes and smog all damned day, he had no misgivings about scrawling his signature.

But now it was time to step up. And here he was, dragging his feet in front of a shop window.

"Get your buck and get out," he muttered, and put his legs in motion.

There was no pretty receptionist waiting today. The Persian fellow greeted him at the unmarked frosted glass door and ushered him into the one-room office, where the only furnishings were a steel desk with a chair on each side and a file cabinet in the corner. Carl didn't need to be psychic to guess the cabinet was empty. The whole place had the look of a temporary operation used for a single discrete purpose.

A tall man with a high shelf of curly black hair rose and reached across the desk to shake his hand. Though Caucasian, he had the stately bearing of a prince, which made Carl feel reluctant to offer his oil-stained fingers. But the man, who introduced himself as "John Parsons, but call me Jack" gave an enthusiastic shake with an eagerness in his bright eyes that suggested the honor was his.

"Have a seat, Mr. Bauman. I'm so pleased you could make it. You're one of just a few select subjects we're following up with."

Carl reconsidered the file cabinet. There was no nurse or equipment in the room—not even a sheet of paper or a deck of cards on the desk. Seated and regarding Parsons across the empty slab, he felt his knee bouncing, a nervous habit, and decided to cut through the bullshit with a direct question. "Is this a drug trial, Mr. Parsons? I read something about fumes on the paper your girl had me sign."

Parsons smiled under a thin mustache, then laughed and swiveled his chair toward his associate, who stood by the window overlooking Wiltshire. "Kamen, you didn't tell Mr. Bauman what to expect?" The other man shrugged. Parsons turned back to Carl and leaned forward, arching an eyebrow and speaking in a conspiratorial tone. "Fumes. That's a word I associate with toxins. You would not believe the fumes *I've* inhaled in the name of science, but that's another story. I've worked in chemical plants, aviation design, rocketry…" He trailed off, then fixed Carl with a reassuring smile and continued. "These days, I'm an associate chemist at USC, but no: It's not fumes or drugs. It's *per*fumes we've asked you here to sample. No need to worry, Mr. Bauman. You did the tarot card exercise for us, right? It's like that. We're interested in what kind of feelings you get from a special blend of incense. It may effect your perception, but that's all. The ingredients are mostly plant products. Are you amenable to that?"

"Will I still get paid no matter what reaction I have?"

"Yes. Of course." Parsons nodded at his partner, who opened a drawer of the file cabinet and removed an object wrapped in white silk, which he unwound to reveal a flat black disc. Parsons produced a brass dish and a charcoal briquette from a desk drawer while the other man set the disk in a wire frame so that it sat upright at the edge of the desk, facing Carl and tilted back at just enough of an angle for him to see his face reflected in the pitch black glass.

"This is an obsidian mirror," Parsons said, "devised by pharaohs for far seeing." His voice had modulated slightly, taking on the resonant tones of a hypnotist.

"Far seeing?"

"Yes. They believed they could see faraway countries, other realms. Heavens and hells and all of their denizens."

"I don't believe in any of that," Carl said. "You don't expect me to pretend I believe in that, do you? You said I still get paid."

"You get paid no matter what you do or don't see in the smoke and glass, Carl. Now I want you to take a deep breath and relax."

There was the sound of a match igniting. Orange sparks sizzled and spit from the charcoal on the brass dish. Parsons pursed his lips and blew air at the burning line until it held steady. Then he produced a glass vial from the pocket of his tweed blazer, uncorked it, and tapped a measure of ochre powder onto the briquette, like a chef adding spice to a stew. Red smoke rose in ribbons, coiling in the air between them. A strange mixture of odors flooded Carl's sinuses: Orchids, ozone, semen, and brine. He couldn't decide if the overall effect was pleasant or not.

"You have no idea how difficult it is," Jack said, "to find someone with no psychic sensitivity."

Carl filled the silence that followed with a nervous laugh. Mr. Parsons had such dark eyes. In the shady room, it was hard to tell where the irises ended and the pupils began. "Is that right?"

"Oh yes. Most people don't realize they're using a sixth sense until you ask about how they make decisions and use their imagination. For most, it's not anything spectacular like having visions. But you...do you see *anything* in the black mirror, Carl? Anything at all?"

Carl shook his head. All he could see was his reflection obscured by the smoke. It was flowing faster now, hanging on the air in layers.

"That's okay," Jack said. "Good, in fact. I didn't expect you would." He laced his fingers together on the desk and tapped his thumbs, watching the play of the incense fumes. "What if I told you it's not a mirror but a window?"

"If it was a window, I'd only see *you* through it."

"But if it was a window to another world—a god realm like the Egyptians claimed—then you'd see the gods gazing back at you."

Carl shifted in the creaky chair. "I don't believe—"

"I know. You said so already. And that's why you can't see past what's in front of your face. I knew a woman who could look into this mirror and see the gods so clearly she could draw their likenesses."

"What happened to her?"

Parsons inhaled deeply. "She went away. We learned a lot together, but she went away and I realized I needed to develop a formula that would draw our neighbors into our world where anyone could see them."

Carl had been to a carnival in Milwaukee once where a mentalist tried to hypnotize him. The man had failed so spectacularly it had set the crowd rolling in their seats. But now he was feeling sleepy, like he could nod right off in the chair. Still, that didn't mean he was going to start hallucinating Egyptian gods if there really wasn't a drug involved. "Why is it red? The smoke."

Parsons smiled. "The scientific reason wouldn't make sense to you, but the poetic answer—if you can *grok* poetry, as my friend Robert says—is that it's like blood in the water, attracting the sharks." The man's dark eyes tracked a scudding plume and he grimaced, appearing to reconsider the analogy. "But poetry only goes so far. The smoke is more than a lure. It grants them substance on our side of the glass, more solid than the form they can take in the imagination of a sensitive host."

The other one was chanting now. Carl wasn't sure when he'd started doing that, but the sound raised the hairs on his sun-scorched forearm.

Parsons' voice pulled his attention back to the mirror. Carl felt sweaty and untethered. Maybe it wasn't worth a dollar after all to sit through this strange talk in the cloying heat with the smell of dead flowers and dusty spices lining his throat. He wanted someone to open a window and offer him a glass of water. These guys weren't scientists. They were batshit. Wait till he told Ray what he'd missed out on by sharing his dreams with them.

"Don't focus on the mirror, Carl. Follow the smoke. Tell us what you see forming in the smoke."

"It's getting solid like." His voice was raspy and distant in his own ears; a voice from the bottom of a well. "Why are you asking me? Can't you see it? It's got ridges now, like a goat's horns."

"I do see it, Carl. But *I* may have a touch of that sixth sense. I want to know that *you* can see it. That it can see you."

And it could see him. The sudden knowledge was like swallowing an icicle. An eye regarded him from the black disk—a throbbing ball of jelly squirming in an electrical storm rimmed with lashes of fang and claw. He noticed the ribbons of smoke wafted not from the brass dish at the base of the mirror, but from that merciless eye. They twisted and billowed and transformed, shrugging off every resemblance his mind grasped for to make sense of them: Spiraling horns, coiling serpent tails, an elephant's trunk, an octopus' tentacle now curling around the back of his neck.

But these appendages were nothing compared to the nexus they led to. Malign and magnetic, it drew him closer with its dark gravity, like the impulse to jump from a great height. Parsons had compared it to a shark, but it was so much worse than that. Even the most fearsome predator was part of a cycle of life, but the thing taking shape in the glass and smoke was beyond nature. Outside. Underneath. And knowing that such things writhed at the rotten core of the world made every thing of beauty on the surface insignificant. He couldn't have articulated these thoughts, but his fraying mind grasped them even as it unspooled and lost the meaning of words, like coins dropped down a storm drain.

"He sees it." The voice was thin and distant, but he still recognized it as Parsons'. Gone now was the measured, hypnotic tone. For Carl Bauman, who would live out the remainder of his days in an asylum, it was the last phrase that would ever carry sense. It reached his ears as the protean limbs embraced him and pulled him in, as if to kiss something surfacing through dark water. Words empty of arrogance, uttered in a tone of rapt fascination.

1

On a cold day in December 1948, Catherine Littlefield followed her usual orbit around a fifteen-ton meteorite at the heart of New York City. She stopped at her dorm room to drop off her books after "Man and the Supernatural" let out, then changed her shoes for the walk to Columbia Street station. Snow had paralyzed the city on Sunday, and while the college's footpaths had been cleared promptly, she was grateful for her waterproof boots on the icy city sidewalks. She took the 1 train to 79th Street and walked a beeline across Columbus Ave to the southwest corner of the American Museum of Natural History. There, she passed through a nondescript archway that led directly into the Hall of the Plains Indians, bypassing the Romanesque grandeur of the Theodore Roosevelt Memorial Hall, and bringing her into the warmth of the brownstone building without delay. She threaded through a group of schoolchildren milling around the canoe just as a ruddy-faced boy fresh from the cold recoiled at the sight of the masked witch-doctor in the prow. He bumped her with his elbow and dropped a fistful of marbles, sending them bouncing across the stone floor in a cascading chaos of echoes. Catherine swept past the admonishing teacher to the end of her weekly pilgrimage: the Hall of the Sun at the Hayden Planetarium, home of the Willamette meteorite.

The Hall itself was a dazzling setting for the rough stone. An illuminated globe that represented the sun hung among models of the planets, revolving and rotating above a marble floor marked with the constellations of the zodiac. But it was the foyer of this grand chamber that drew her like a moth to a flame, where a hulk of cratered iron the size of a DeSoto taxicab rested on a block of granite flanked by a pair of benches. The largest meteorite ever found in the United States.

Catherine perched on the same bench as always, a vantage from which she watched children climb the mammoth rock and fit their petite bodies into its nooks and crannies with a mixture of awe and horror. For her part, she kept to a safe distance despite her fascination. Close enough to feel the hum it emitted, but far enough away that she could form coherent thoughts and recall her own name, even though she had promised herself she wouldn't give it to the man in the gray overcoat if he finally asked.

He was there again today, waiting for her in the entry hall of the Hayden, sitting on the bench opposite the one she favored. The first time she'd noticed him, he'd been standing in a corner behind a cluster of schoolchildren. In the weeks that had elapsed since then, he had gradually grown bolder, approaching her domain like a hunter who has abandoned stealth in closing the final yards to his prey.

Catherine had left her own coat at the checkroom, as she always did, whether visiting the research library on the fifth floor for homework or the meteor for... What? What exactly did she come here for? Psychic sustenance? The taste of the numinous she'd failed to find in the Baptist Church of her ancestors in prosaic Newburyport, Massachusetts? Or perhaps proof there was more to the universe than could be analyzed in ancient texts and mounted in glass cases? All she was sure of at nineteen was this: of the many and varied cathedrals New York City had on offer, the Museum of Natural History had become her church, and the Willamette meteorite her altar.

She smoothed her skirt and closed her eyes and had just settled in to meditate on the hum that no other visitor seemed to hear when the man in the gray coat finally spoke.

"You can feel it, can't you? Even though you never touch it."

Catherine opened her eyes. His bearded face hovered beyond the contours of the rock. He rose and moved around it, his eyes intent upon hers—dark, but not without a flicker of kindness. Or was it curiosity?

"Do you know what they call it? The Indians who worshipped it before it was brought here?"

Feeling exposed in the beam of the man's gaze, she longed for her coat. She shook her head, the slightest of gestures.

"*Tomanowos*. It's a Chinook word. You may have passed their artifacts on your way here. It means, *spiritual power*."

Catherine didn't doubt this man knew exactly what path she took on her visits. Did he also watch from some shadow on the days when she took the elevator to the fifth floor for research? Had he ever stalked her on campus? The notion gave her a chill, but there was nothing lascivious in his gaze. Rather, what she saw in the lines around his eyes was the academic interest of a scholar encountering a rare specimen in the field.

But how did he know? How *could* he unless he felt it, too?

"They worshipped it. Before the white man wrapped it in chains and put it on a truck to New York. Now children with no sense of its power treat it like a Jungle Gym."

He drew a breath and broke eye contact. Was she giving him the hard stare her father was always commenting on? There was sadness in his eyes, but not shame. Voices ricocheted along the granite walls of the corridor, but for now, they were alone. The stranger's eyes focused on the stone as he continued his lecture.

"The Clackamas tribe of the Willamette Valley considered it an emissary of the sky people. They collected rainwater from its crevices, which they drank as a healing tonic. Warriors anointed arrowheads with the holy water to imbue them with power."

He settled on the bench beside Catherine. "When the settlers on the Oregon Trail moved the tribes to reservations, the meteorite went unnoticed until a Welsh immigrant found it and tried to make a buck off it. That was 1902. The Oregon Iron and Steel Company almost decided to melt it down for raw material."

Catherine felt her face betraying shock at the thought. The man leaned forward, nodding his head and lacing his fingers around his knee. He wore a gold signet ring on the middle finger of his right hand, graven with a symbol that resembled a tree branch with five prongs. It tickled a memory. Something she had read. But whether she'd come across it in her academic work or her private obsession with secret societies, she couldn't recall.

"A piece of a shattered planet's core, crashed to earth and traveled on an iceberg down a flooded valley at the end of an ice age, and they were going to melt it down for raw material. We have a rich widow to thank for its preservation. Sarah Dodge bought the meteorite for a small fortune and donated it to the museum for all mankind to share."

The voices of the schoolchildren had moved beyond the doors of the auditorium, and for a moment it felt as though she and this man whose name she didn't know, who insisted on giving her an education she hadn't asked for, might be the only two souls in all of the museum. Meteorites were not her field of study; she was an anthropology student. And yet she found herself riveted, hanging on his every word.

"Thousands have seen it since we acquired it in 1906. But few have possessed the sensitivity to sense its raw power."

"You said 'we.' Do you work for the planetarium?"

"Forgive me." The man extended his hand and she took it. His skin was soft, though his ring chilled her fingers. She felt a tingle at the touch, a subtle but almost physical vibration. "Walter Hildebrand. Curator of the Hall of Minerals and Gems. And whom do I have the pleasure of meeting?"

"Catherine." She stopped short of speaking her last name, though she suspected he already knew it. "I'm sure I don't know what you mean about *feeling* something, except that it sounds like superstition, if you'll pardon my candor."

Her bluff elicited a wry grin. "Touch it then," he said, gesturing at the stone. "Go on."

She stood and moved away from the bench, her back to the empty corridor. She had only his word that he was on the museum staff. He came to his feet, stepped forward, and laid a hand on the meteorite. Catherine held her breath. When nothing happened, she realized she'd expected a reaction from the man, or even from the rock itself—a flash of light or a modulation of the vibration thrumming in her chest. But why should there be? People touched the thing all day long.

"I feel it," he said, answering the silent question that hung between them. "I can attenuate it. Not the power it radiates, but my sensitivity to it. At the risk of sounding like a spiritualist, I've strengthened my aura, tempered it like a plate of armor. I could teach you. If you care to learn."

Curiosity and nerve were not qualities Catherine Littlefield had ever been accused of lacking, but there were times when she felt more like a girl far from home than the intrepid anthropologist she intended to become. And this was one of them. It was too much. The hall was her sacred place, and though it was often crowded with the unwitting, what she felt here, in the rock's presence, had belonged to her alone. Until now.

Without a parting word, she turned and fled, her footsteps slapping echoes off the walls until she was cloaked in the anonymity of the exhibit halls, drifting among the tourists, in the shadow of a giant squid suspended above the milling crowd.

2

If not for the signet ring, Catherine would have tried to avoid further encounters with Walter Hildebrand. Her academic work was accumulating like the snow on the ground for every hour she'd spent mesmerized by the Willamette meteorite, so the presence of a stalker was all the reason she needed to cut the distraction out of her routine. But when she tried to focus on her books and banish the man from her mind, the symbol nagged at her, setting off a chain of associations. From a branch etched in gold to the Golden Bough to the Germanic etymological roots of the man's name. Before long, she was digging through books that had nothing to do with her course work, reading about Rosicrucians, Theosophists, poets, and pagans. And so it was that she found herself lurking behind a plaster cast of a monolithic Easter Island head on the eve of the winter solstice, spying on the Hall of Minerals and Gems from the relative darkness of the Pacific Peoples exhibit.

She'd spent the previous evening lurking around the fifth floor administrative wing on the pretext of visiting the library and had followed Hildebrand from a discrete distance when he left his office at 4:45. He'd taken the stairs down to the fourth floor for a final sweep through the long rows of glass cases in the Hall of Minerals and Gems before leaving work for the day. If that was characteristic of his daily routine, she could pick up his trail here again. Something about the man told her he was meticulous. When she checked her watch and saw it was already 4:50 with no sign of him, she considered hurrying across the hall and taking the elevator to the ground floor to watch the exit. But in the spacious Roosevelt Hall, she couldn't count on a crowd to conceal her this late on a weekday. At least from her hideout behind the statue, she could be sure of trailing behind him. *If* he appeared.

She checked her watch again. It was a silver art deco piece that her parents gave her for graduation: 4:56. She told herself that no matter how methodical a man was, things came up that might keep him at his desk late. Phone calls and loose ends. If she had time to monitor his routine for a week, she might gain the confidence to trust in it, but her gut told her she didn't have a week. Today was the solstice, and if his ring indicated the affiliation she suspected, it had to be tonight when she followed him. It was only an intuition, but a strong one, and she'd learned long ago to trust her hunches. They seemed to originate in the same part of her mind that was sensitive to the energy radiating from the meteorite in the corridor three floors below.

Catherine was preparing herself for the possibility of being spotted by her prey crossing the span of well-lit glass cabinets and white pillars when a long, gray overcoat came into view, moving briskly around a corner and up a row to her left toward the Origins of Man exhibit.

A drop of perspiration traced a rivulet from behind her ear to the scarf draped around her neck. She exhaled softly and waited for him to reach the shadows of the adjacent hall, then followed.

When he took the elevator, she took the stairs, a jaunt that left her short of breath and overheated in her winter attire by the time she reached the bottom.

He left the museum via the exit onto Central Park West. Catherine was grateful for the early dark of December when the closing time crowd carried her out onto the wide stone steps, though it did nothing to conceal her as she crossed the street with a thinning number. Fortunately, Hildebrand did not look back, allowing her to follow his dusky coat into the trees.

The snow on the ground caught the light of the footpath lamps, extending the radius of illumination and requiring her to keep a greater distance than she would have liked. She almost lost him near the triple-arch stone bridge, but was able to pick up his tracks in the snow, having noted their size and shape at the start of her pursuit. Soon they were wending a course through the Ramble—the tangle of woods that skirted the lake.

The ring suggested membership in the Order of the Golden Bough, a secret society devoted to ceremonial magic and mysticism. Little was known of their initiation ceremonies and teachings, but some scholars theorized that they were influenced by the ancient priest-kings of Nemi, guardians of the sacred tree beside the lake known as Diana's mirror in Rome, as reconstructed by Sir James George Frazer.

Hiding behind the Moai head in the warmth of the museum, Catherine had clung to this theory with conviction. But now, in the cold and dark, creeping among the tangled shadows of tree and branch, doubt crept in. Overgrown and secluded, the Ramble had a reputation for homosexual trysts. She imagined it was too cold for that on the darkest day of the year, but what if she was following him to such an encounter?

If so, she would retreat quietly, she decided, unsure if it would be a disappointment or a relief. Her boots were serving her well, but already her fingers were going numb. She squeezed her hands together, trying to get the blood circulating, and plodded onward, grateful that the snow at least masked the sound of her footsteps.

Away from the lamps that lined the paved paths, Catherine's eyes acclimated to the darkness. Above the lake, the waning moon conspired with the skyscrapers to blot out the stars. She waited in the shelter of a shelf of rock for Hildebrand to reach the top of a rise, then followed quickly when he disappeared down the other side. At the crest, she looked down and caught her breath. His silhouette descended toward a ring of candles that sent waves of yellow light lapping at the base of a gnarled oak. At the fringes of the circle of light, a group of masked figures in overcoats stood motionless.

The white masks reflected enough candlelight to resemble alabaster animal faces, their details blurred by distance. Was one in the shape of an eagle's beak? Did the curling lines of another represent the mane of a lion?

Hildebrand showed no reluctance to approach the figures, and as the assembly parted to make room for him, Catherine watched his shadow stretch to take on the horns of a bull. When had he donned a mask? And where had he concealed it before? He'd carried no briefcase or bag. She crouched low and strained to hear over the wind rising off the lake, whistling in the bare branches. But no sound reached her from the congregation until Hildebrand joined their ranks and a bell chimed from some unseen quarter.

A hooded man was thrust into the circle with a shove that sent him to his knees. Catherine had crept close enough to see his hands were bound with rough rope behind his back. The black hood covering his head was tied with another length of rope, which trailed in the snow behind him. She could see his breath moving the hood where his mouth would be. The one who had thrust him forward stepped back, his mask that of a dog, fangs frozen in a perpetual grimace. Catherine was reminded of the ceremonial masks on display at the museum, the varied forms the witch doctors wore: birds and bears and the disk of the sun. Embodiments of the energies encountered in mankind's dance around the seasonal wheel. This pageantry was surely another incarnation of the same drama, staged by and for the spiritual edification of well-to-do academics. She told herself this, but it did nothing to soothe the anxiety churning in her stomach at the sight of the ropes, the hood, and the sword that now emerged from the shadow of the dog man's coat, pulling a blazing line of the scant light to its keen blade like a magnet.

There was a glint of gold, and she saw that the man in the sacrificial victim role—she was still certain it must be a role—wore a thin crown atop the black hood. A twisted vine twined between the gold prongs. She couldn't be sure, but it looked like mistletoe.

Hildebrand stepped into the circle now, the shadow of his mask's horns stretching out before him in the ashen snow. The sword hovered inches above the kneeling man's neck while Hildebrand recited a verse in a rolling baritone she wouldn't have thought him capable of:

From where the Witch's Fortress
O'er hangs the dark-blue seas;
From the still glassy lake that sleeps
Beneath Aricia's trees—
Those trees in who's dim shadow
The ghastly priest doth reign,
The priest who slew the slayer,

And shall himself be slain.

The dog man touched the blade to the back of the man's neck, causing him to flinch as if the blade had transmitted an electrical shock. Then he hefted it aloft, poised for the killing stroke. The condemned didn't beg or struggle to gain his feet, and Catherine thought again that it must be theater. But for what audience?

The sword swept downward. She screamed, "Stop!" and the blade veered off its trajectory, swishing the fabric of the executioner's coat where it came to rest at the end of its arc.

The masks turned toward her in unison. Could they see her face among the shadows? She considered running, but they were already upon her, the dog and eagle seizing her by the arms and dragging her into the light.

Dark eyes regarded her through the bull mask. Hildebrand. A foot came down on the back of her leg, buckling her knee and dropping her to the frozen ground. She turned to the victim who knelt beside her. White-gloved hands removed the crown from his head. A second pair grasped the rope around his neck and tugged at the noose, loosening it. His head swiveled toward her as the hood was tugged away to reveal not a face but another mask. This one didn't resemble an animal, but a frowning man rendered in the same archetypal style, waves of alabaster hair swept back from a high brow and impassive blue eyes twinkling in the candlelight. She saw no gratitude there, only a cold curiosity. Then he rose to his feet and stepped away, and Catherine felt the cold metal of the crown placed upon her own head.

The poem echoed in her mind, teasing some recollection that wouldn't come. She'd heard it before but couldn't place it in context under duress. She drew a deep breath and struggled to calm her mind. Her senses heightened by fear, she heard every rustle of fabric, every shuffle of shoes as the officers of the ritual adjusted their positions around her to the mournful whistle of the wind in the trees. She felt cold to the core, but a strange calm settled on her mind as she watched the shining sword rising in her peripheral vision. A delicate rumble of thunder resounded from somewhere in the trees.

Holding her breath, she heard a voice that might have been Hildebrand—*One, two, three…Let the Queen headless be!*—followed by the rasp of steel ripping the air. She forced herself not to flinch. The slice terminated in a clang and the crown tumbled from her head, taking a lock of her hair with it. Red strands fell to the snow in the center of a gold circle braided with leaves and berries.

Sensing a shift in the positions of those around her, she looked up. The dog presented the sword to the bull. Images from tarot cards and paintings flickered through her reeling mind. Dogs as guardians of the threshold. Mithras, the bull-headed god, as hierophant, initiator. The four evangelists of the Bible as Lion, Bull, Eagle, and Man. Had she really just gambled her life in Central Park, two hundred miles from her home and parents, surrounded by a gang of men with a blade? Bet it on an anthropological hunch about the nature of their game?

Yes, she supposed she had. Laughter bubbled up in her chest at the thought. Only the intensity of Hildebrand's eyes—if that was even his real name—helped her to suppress it.

He raised the sword, but this time in a non-threatening ceremonial gesture, and she knew what he was about to do. He touched the flat of the blade to each of her shoulders in turn. "Catherine Littlefield, daughter of Gerald, I grant thee entrance unto the outer circle. Do you swear to serve the order with fealty and to guard its secrets with your life?"

"I do."

"Do you accept that should you reveal the mystic teachings or the true identities of your brethren, you shall face the sword a second time?"

Knowing it would be impossible to reveal the identities of masked men, she nodded. "I do." Two syllables that felt reckless, impulsive, and exhilarating. A blind marriage. She had long dreamed of finding fellow seekers, of being initiated into their ranks, but it had always seemed like a dim and distant possibility, and if there was anything she feared in that moment, it was that the secrets wouldn't live up to the proffered penalty. No sooner had the words passed her lips than the candles went dark. The scent of burning bee's wax wafted past her on a curling wisp of smoke.

"Rise, my child."

Her knees had gone numb from the cold, and she wavered as she came up on her feet. Hildebrand offered a steadying hand. When she met his eyes, she was surprised to see his bearded face smiling back at her. The mask and sword were gone. They were alone, the two of them, beneath the boughs of the great oak. Alone in moonlight, with no sign on the ground that any others had been in attendance, or that a pagan initiation rite had reached its climax just a moment ago.

"Where…"

"Home. Back to their lives. In the outer circle, you will only know the one who brought you in. Later, when you've passed the second gate, you will meet them again without their masks."

"You knew I would follow you."

"I *hoped* you would."

"It was a test."

"Only the brave and curious are granted entrance."

"I wasn't brave when you approached me at the museum."

"You were cautious. The meteorite is a measure of sensitivity, the first requirement. There are other locations and objects that serve the same function, but it is the most powerful, and I have the honor of watching it. Sometimes it draws moths. Of those, some possess the daring to become butterflies."

"I think it's caterpillars that become butterflies, professor."

His beard twitched with a grin. "I'm not a professor. Just a curator."

"Well, you remind me of one. Even if you don't know much about butterflies."

This earned her a raised eyebrow. They were back on a paved footpath by now, lit by intermittent lamps. "They're not brave," she said. "Mostly, they just sort of meander around."

Striding ahead with purpose, Hildebrand spoke without looking back at her. "Monarchs from New England fly all the way to Mexico, where they are welcomed on the Day of the Dead. Now *that's* daring."

She paused at a fork in the path. "Where are you going?" He had taken the branch that led deeper into the park. "It's this way back to the street."

"Follow and find out, if you dare."

Catherine watched his gray coat dissolve into a patch of shadows. An old hermetic axiom surfaced in her mind: *To know, to will, to dare, and to keep silent*. She was cold. It was late. The park was closed, a haunt for the criminal and transgressive until sunrise. But she had already shouted at a coven of masked men and knelt beneath a sword tonight. Maybe the risky part of her evening was behind her. She tucked her scarf into her coat and followed, unaware that the biggest risk she underestimated was that of her own impulsiveness, and that she might yet agree to further adventure.

3

Hildebrand moved fast, and Catherine's initial hesitation allowed a good distance to unspool between them as she trailed his silhouette along the winding path that skirted the Turtle Pond. By the time she'd lost sight of him, the lights of the Metropolitan Museum of Art glimmered through the trees, and she guessed where he must be leading her. Sure enough, when she crested the knoll and arrived at the Egyptian obelisk, she found him sitting on the iron railing that surrounded it, his back to the path.

His posture was meditative, his head level, not tilted up toward the towering stone monument. Approaching him, she was startled to find his coat draped over the railing at his side, his fingers interlaced in a mudra in his lap, and his white dress shirt streaming vapor into the brisk air. Stepping over the railing, she saw that the shirt was soaked through with sweat. His eyes remained closed, though he must have heard her. His chest rose and fell in a slow, deep rhythm. As she sat beside him, she felt a tingle of *deja vu*. Or was it just symmetry? Here they were again, sitting on a bench of sorts, looking at a giant, ancient rock. But really, she was looking at him, and he was looking within.

He broke the intricate hand gesture and patted the folded overcoat. "Put this on, please. You could use another layer."

She unfolded the coat and slipped it over her shoulders. They'd been outside long enough that the cold had crept under her skin, but it helped. Watching the steam rise from his shirt, she opened her mouth, but he answered the question before she could ask it.

"It's a modified Tibetan technique. *Tum-mo,* the yoga of inner fire. First taught among men at Nalanda University in India, around the second century."

"Among men?" It seemed like an odd qualifier. Few of the ancient mysteries were ever taught to women. She'd learned that in grade school when she expressed an interest in the Masonic temple in Newburyport.

"Legend has it that the first yogi to master the technique learned it from the *nagas*—snake people from a submarine kingdom in the Indian Ocean."

"Do you believe that?"

He took one of her hands in his. Heat poured through her thin wool gloves and she almost pulled them back in shock. But it felt good, and she relaxed, allowing herself to soak up both the heat and the tactile evidence of a minor miracle.

"I have no reason to doubt it," he said. "There are more things in heaven and earth—and under the sea I dare say…"

"Than are dreamt of in your philosophy," she finished, and released his hands.

He nodded at the obelisk. "What do you know about it?"

"It was a gift to New York from Egypt, brought here in 1880 to much fanfare. It stands sixty-nine feet tall, and the inscription is the usual sort of thing—praise to the king who commissioned it. Thutmosis the third. 'He is god incarnate and the scythe in his hand slew the enemies of Egypt and expanded the kingdom, etcetera.'"

Hildebrand gave her a sidelong glance. "Not bad."

"I'm pursuing a minor in ancient languages."

He acknowledged this with a nod.

"And I read the brochure when I visited the Met."

Was that a smile in the dark? Hildebrand rolled a hand, an invitation for more, if she had it.

She gathered what little else she knew and delivered it in one long breath. "It originally had a twin. That one is now installed in London. The name, Cleopatra's Needle, has no basis in Egyptian history. It was picked up along the way when the Romans moved the obelisk to Alexandria, where it languished in the dirty trade port until a corrupt politician decided making a gift of it might improve trade relations with America."

"Impressive. But again, not much more than you could find in a brochure."

"I've always wondered about the crabs," Catherine said. Giant iron crabs braced the eroded lower corners of the obelisk where it met the stone base.

"These crabs are replicas of a set forged by the Romans, apparently in reference to the sun god, Apollo," he said. "I've never found that to be a very satisfying explanation for them."

"Why not?"

Hildebrand shrugged. "I'm unable to find other references to crabs as sacred to Apollo. Dolphins would make more sense."

She squeezed her hands between her thighs to warm them. "So tell me: why are we here at midnight on the darkest day of the year?"

"You're right about Thutmosis, the third. He commissioned it. But an additional inscription was added on the north side under Ramses the Great: *The crowned Horus, Bull of Victory, Son of Khephra.*"

Catherine thought of the bull mask Hildebrand had worn earlier and decided to try and coax him out of obscurity with willful ignorance. "That may be in praise of a different pharaoh, but it's the same old song. Identification with the sun god."

"Perhaps. And who is Khephra?"

"The scarab beetle who carries the sun through the underworld."

"There is a legend of an artifact, a golden scarab that holds a fiery red gem in its pincers."

"And gems are your area of expertise..." Catherine had spent little time in the Hall of Minerals and Gems. Just enough to come away convinced that anyone who visited the museum owed it to themselves to see the Star of India sapphire and the DeLong star ruby. They were wonders of nature.

"This jewel has given birth to countless legends. It is said to be a weapon against dark gods, creatures from the stars whose presence on earth predated the emergence of man. Some accounts claim it was last used during the reign of Ramses the Great, and that the ancient adepts may have hid it away in the base of an obelisk for a day when those forces would pierce the veil and walk the earth again. One of those dark gods even bears the claws of a crab."

Hildebrand walked to the north face of the obelisk. "The Ramses inscription continues: *Like the orb of the Sun, when he shines in the horizon, the lord of the Two Lands.*"

"Upper and Lower Egypt," Catherine said.

"That would be the obvious interpretation—the exoteric, so to speak. The *esoteric* reading, favored by our order, is that this refers to two adjacent worlds, planes of existence, or dimensions. The scarab, the *Fire of Cairo,* could travel between these worlds, like the 'orb of the sun.' and burn the dark gods with its rays."

"That's why you perform initiations near the obelisk. The Golden Bough considers it a sacred site because you believe a magic jewel lies hidden in the foundation." She could scarcely believe she was articulating such an outlandish theory, but his intimations all pointed to that one conclusion.

"Many members of our fraternity through the ages have also been Brothers of the Craft. The obelisk itself was transported across the ocean and raised here by Freemasons. Henry Hurlbolt Gorringe, the brother in charge of that herculean endeavor, arranged for a small box to be included in a time capsule set into the base of the monument. The other contents of the capsule are well documented, but Gorringe alone knew the contents of the box."

"And you think the scarab is in there. As you believe it was in Egypt."

He met her eyes. "I *hope* it is. I want to believe, to know."

"Was Gorringe also a member of the Golden Bough?"

Hildebrand let his gaze climb the pillar of stone, relying on silence to maintain his vow.

"If the scarab was such a vital weapon… Didn't he tell anyone in the order? Or leave a written record of what was in the box?"

Hildebrand sighed. "None we can find. He was trying to protect something that had remained hidden for centuries, and may have placed it where it might only be retrieved in the event of an apocalypse. But I don't believe he would have taken that secret to the grave willingly. He thought there would be time. He was wrong. He survived a shipwreck and lived as a castaway as a boy, served in the navy, and lived a lifetime of adventures abroad, but was killed in a freak accident at the age of forty-four trying to board a moving train. Of course, we've always suspected he was the victim of a curse."

Catherine scoffed. She couldn't help it. "An ancient Egyptian curse, like the death of Lord Carnarvon? The curse of King Tut's tomb? It was a mosquito bite that got *him*, you know."

"Not an ancient curse. A modern one, by a rival group who would like for the amulet to remain lost to history. The Starry Wisdom Church."

All her life, Catherine had heard rumors of the cult. They were said to have chapters in Rhode Island and Massachusetts and some affiliation with the Esoteric Order of Dagon in her own ancestral neck of the woods. She remembered a priestess' diadem, still on display in a glass case at the Newburyport Historical Society on High Street. It has always fascinated her as a rare relic of feminine spiritual leadership.

"All this talk about brotherhoods," she said. "The masked figures were men tonight. Are there other women in the order?"

"You are the first."

She had suspected as much, but didn't know if she should feel honored or afraid now that he'd confirmed it. "Why me? Why now?"

Hildebrand's dark eyes swept over her. "If you wish to proceed to the next gate, you must perform a task for the order. Like the Monarch, you must fly to a far away land."

"Mexico?"

"California. We've heard reports of Starry Wisdom activity there that concern us. There is a man, a mage who may have acquired dangerous materials. We have reason to hope he might spill his secrets to you, if you can earn his trust."

"Again: Why me?"

Hildebrand shrugged. "He has a thing for redheads."

She shook her head. "So it's biology, then. Not anthropology. I should have known."

"You decline?"

"I didn't say that. What's *his* specialty?"

"Rocketry."

4

Catherine had never heard of Jack Parsons. A thirty-four-year-old engineer living in Redondo Beach, California, he'd made headlines in the west coast papers ten years ago for providing expert testimony in a Los Angeles car bombing trial. His life's work—building rocket engines—had earned him little fame outside of Cal Tech and the Department of Defense, where he was a pioneer. But if widespread recognition for his accomplishments had eluded him, notoriety had not. The man who'd developed the first solid-fuel jet engine to enable high-speed lift-off from tropical island airfields during the war was better known for his obsessions with sex, drugs, and black magic.

Hildebrand briefed Catherine on their subject over tea and pie at a diner on the park after their visit to Cleopatra's Needle. Most of his information came from a member of the Golden Bough who had infiltrated the Ordo Templi Orientis—the rival order to which Parsons belonged, presided over until recently by the now deceased British magician, Aleister Crowley.

Catherine was intellectually prepared for the information she was now privy to, but felt emotionally out of her depth. Drinking tea with a man who had donned an animal mask and held a sword above her head mere hours ago, listening to his tales of the orgies and explosives engineered by the madman he wanted her to get close to...it was as if she'd turned a page of her life expecting to find a society of academics enacting dramatic rituals only to find herself hip-deep in a spy novel where real magicians could heat their bodies like coals and amulets forged for ancient pharaohs lay buried under Central Park. As the story unfolded, it occurred to her that maybe the obelisk was aptly named after all. The thread of her life had passed through its eye tonight—and now it was pulling her into a tapestry she could never have imagined a year ago.

Parsons had recently been investigated by the FBI for communist affiliations going back to his early days at Cal Tech. Such scrutiny was not unusual for engineers involved in military work. Anyone who owned a television knew that the House Committee on Un-American Activities was busy stoking the fires of suspicion, scouring Hollywood for potential traitors. The national perception of Russia had shifted from wartime ally to global aggressor in the wake of Stalin's invasion of Czechoslovakia, and for Parsons—whose social circles were a three-ring circus of bohemians, science-fiction writers, and occultists—the investigation resulted in the loss of his job on the Navaho Missile Program when his security clearance was revoked. Soon after, his wife returned from a trip to Europe where she'd learned of Crowley's death and found Parsons pumping gas to make ends meet. She responded by running off to join an artist's colony in Mexico.

The lost security clearance turned out to be a temporary setback. A friend petitioned for reinstatement while Parsons made the case that the OTO was a non-political religious organization. When the government restored his credentials, he found employment at the Hughes Aircraft Corporation.

"Are you sure *you* don't work for the FBI, Mr. Hildebrand? For a Manhattan gemologist, you know an awful lot about this rocketeer from Pasadena. Or does the order have spies everywhere?"

Hildebrand smiled and refilled his cup from the small steel kettle the waitress had left on the table. "Our numbers are few, though we maintain lodges in several countries."

"You'd have to be as big as the Freemasons to zero in on a single individual on the other side of the country."

"We've been very resourceful where Mr. Parsons is concerned. He is of the utmost interest to us."

"Resourceful enough even to recruit a girl."

"Other women have helped us learn of his activities."

Catherine raised an eyebrow.

"Since his wife's departure, Jack has employed prostitutes to aid in his sex magic operations."

Catherine gathered her purse and slid out from behind the table, her face flushed with heat. "I'm afraid I misjudged you and your associates. You've certainly misjudged me."

Hildebrand reached for her arm, but withdrew his hand at the sight of her withering glare. "Please, Catherine. I didn't mean to imply… Please, sit and hear me out."

"What, exactly, didn't you mean to imply? You told me plainly that he likes redheads. You initiated me for my gender. I'm so stupid. I let your little body heat trick dazzle me into thinking you had wisdom to offer, but I should have known better. Your secrets are the usual tawdry kind."

"That's not true. You're the first woman ever admitted past the first gate. You were selected for your sensitivity, your talent. And you have no idea what it took for me to convince them."

"Them?"

"My superiors."

"How am I the first if you have Hollywood call girls in your ranks?"

Hildebrand looked aghast. It would have been comical if she weren't so furious. "Not as *initiates*. Dear God, no. We've merely paid some of Jack's ladies for whatever details we can glean from their testimony. The content of his rituals and what they've seen at his house—books and artifacts we fear he may have acquired. But they lack the knowledge to recognize or retain most of the details we're interested in. They're mostly good for reporting on pillow talk about his mundane life, his career, and marital woes. We might get lucky if one can draw a symbol he painted on her body, or remember a word he taught her to chant until the sun came up, but that's not enough to reconstruct his operations. For anything more esoteric, we've had to rely on whatever Parsons has been willing to share with our primary contact, an exiled high priest of the OTO. And that's not enough. Will you please sit? People will think I'm accosting you."

Catherine put her purse back down and settled beside it, at the edge of the seat. She adjusted her watch on the wrist he had grabbed. It reminded her of her parents and how far from home she was. "You've got one minute to tell me what you expect me to do, or you can keep your second gate closed and forget I ever crossed the first."

"Jack is dabbling with dangerous forces. He's indiscriminate—unable to tell the difference between harmless superstition and truly apocalyptic lines of inquiry. He's attracted to darkness—"

"Forty seconds."

"We need someone who knows what to look for. With Marjorie—his wife—out of the picture, there's an opportunity to reach him, and yes, if he finds you attractive, it will help you slip past his defenses, but it's only conversation we're asking you to engage in."

"You said he's practicing sex magic."

"And we're not asking you to take part. The last thing we want is to further his pursuits. We fear he's done enough harm already. But we need to assess how much. I would train you before sending you out there, so you're aware of what to look for and what questions to ask, if he takes you under his wing. It would be dangerous work, but we will take every precaution to protect you. There are hermetic practices that would reinforce your aura, provide you with psychic armor of a sort. And we have allies you could turn to in California, if you needed to flee."

"What does this have to do with the amulet buried under the obelisk?"

"Again, we can't be sure it's there. If it is, it may be best to let it lie beneath a few hundred tons of stone until such a day as the city falls. There are cultists who would seek to destroy the scarab and would kill to obtain it. The time may come when the Fire of Cairo is our last defense against the Great Old Ones. If Jack Parsons can be diverted from the work he is pursuing, we may prevent a catastrophe: A trans-dimensional incursion. Prophesy heralds its arrival, but perhaps not in this century. And should you manage to retrieve a certain book we fear Parsons has acquired, we would be better prepared for the dreaded day when it comes."

"What book?"

"*The Mortiferum Indicium*, or 'Deadly Amulet.' It describes the scarab's functions and powers, its origins, and the mantras that activate it. Like most grimoires, it has been passed down in fragmentary forms and bastardized translations. The copy Parsons may possess was once the property of Henry Hurlbolt Gorringe, stolen with his briefcase by a member of the Starry Wisdom cult when he tripped and fell from the train platform."

"There was a branch of the Starry Wisdom near where I grew up, in Newburyport. But no one knew what they worshipped."

"They prefer to keep it that way. Their gods are monsters. Their holy books are summoning manuals."

"Why then would they want a book about a weapon that could threaten their gods?"

"To aid them in recognizing the threat if it were one day recovered."

"And is Parsons actually summoning these Old Gods? Evoking them to physical manifestation?"

"Not quite. Not yet. He lives in a concrete castle overlooking the beach, but if he'd called something like that up, if he'd brought it through from the other side, there would be no hiding it. We would have no need of spies. His neighbors—any who survived the event—would know. For now, if our sources are correct, he is limited to communing with the gods through a relic of the Starry Wisdom Church, an obsidian mirror upon which the black pharaoh Nephren-ka exhaled his dying breath. Parsons would have obtained both the book and the mirror from an acolyte of the church named Abdelmalek, a mathematics student at Cal Tech."

"How does the mirror work?"

"It's a window to the other side. But a window only, not a door."

"And Parsons just happened to meet someone who had possession of it? At a technical college."

Hildebrand grinned at his teacup and took a sip. "You'll find that initiates don't believe in coincidences."

"Then you're suggesting that members of the Starry Wisdom have been surveilling Parsons the same as you. Using him to further their plans." Catherine laughed. Her slice of pie was gone. She picked up a crumb of crust and popped it into her mouth. Not very ladylike, but she was famished. It had been a long night. "Between the government, the Golden Bough, and the Starry Wisdom, is there a minute of the day when someone *isn't* spying on Jack Parsons? I'm surprised you aren't all bumping into each other."

"That's a real risk. And why we need someone to get closer."

"So your adversaries planted someone in Jack's orbit to ensure that these occult objects fell into his hands. Why?"

"Among the initiated, there is a feeling that the Second World War ushered in a new age. In the winter of 1945 to 46, Parsons and an associate named L. Ron Hubbard engaged in a series of rituals derived from the Enochian system of magic, intended to evoke what he called an 'elemental mate.' This, mind you, was after Jack's companion Betty, the sister of his first wife, had left him for Hubbard. For a time, they all lived in Jack's rundown mansion in Pasadena."

"That sounds like an incestuous hive."

"You don't know the half of it. In any event, several weeks of evocation reached a climax at an intersection of power lines in the Mohave Desert, where the rocket scientist declared to the science fiction writer that the operation was completed. Upon returning home, Parson found a striking redhead named Marjorie Cameron on his doorstep. She'd heard about the commune from a friend, but Jack believed she'd been sent by the gods."

"Is this the wife you mentioned who recently left for Mexico?"

"Indeed. She goes by 'Candy' among her friends. She had no interest in the occult until Jack cultivated it. Her ambition was to be an artist, and with Jack's guidance, she has produced a terrifying portfolio. Our friend in the OTO set eyes on a few of her sketches. Apparently Jack spent a solid month conjuring Great Old Ones in the obsidian mirror while Marjorie committed their alien anatomy to paper."

The electric heater beside the table had slowly driven the chill from Catherine's bones, but now it crept back in.

"She is gifted with a certain sensitivity."

"Like mine, with the meteorite?"

Hildebrand nodded. "Do you see now why we feel that your mind is of greater value than your body in this endeavor?"

Catherine wrapped her cold hands around her cup. "I'm a student. I can't just skip town for California."

"Parsons appears to be in a dormant phase after furious activity over the past few months. Candy is out of the country, and the stars won't be right for him to resume his experiments until summer, which gives us ample time to prepare you."

"I'm expected home for the summer. What will I tell my parents?"

He shrugged. It was hard to tell with the beard, but she thought he might be struggling to suppress a smile. "Tell them you've been offered an internship."

5

Catherine's roommate was asleep when she let herself in later that night and gone by the time she woke the next morning. She didn't find the note on her desk until she was packing her basket with books for her nine o'clock Study of Unwritten Languages class. Sarah's typically meticulous cursive was sloppy enough to give Catherine a pang of guilt at the thought of her scrawling the message half-asleep in the depths of the night.

Peter called.
TWICE

The pang of guilt only lasted for a second, and the tingle of anticipation that followed it surprised her. She'd first met the wiry, blue-eyed Columbia med student at a beatnik poetry reading Sarah dragged her to in November. Catherine and Peter had bonded over their mutual disdain for the material (he was dragged along by the lit major Sarah was dating). Catherine had seen him three times since—once at a party and then on two dates: a movie, and a tour she'd given him of the museum that maybe didn't count. She'd been tempted to show him the Willamette meteorite, just to see if he had any reaction to it, but steered clear of it at the last minute for fear it might befuddle her in front of him. Raised on a farm in Rochester County, he seemed more awkward and out of place in the big city than most students, but he possessed a modest charm, free of artifice, that appealed to her.

The movie date had left her with little hope he would call again. In hindsight, she supposed if she'd picked a more romantic film, maybe *The Red Shoes*, things might have gone differently. But no, she had to suggest *The Snake Pit*, a dark drama starring Olivia de Havilland that chronicled a woman's stay in a mental institution. It was good, if unsettling. Catherine had read the book the film was based on and hoped the realistic depiction of mental illness might appeal to an aspiring doctor, but they'd spent their coffee afterward searching for other things to talk about, leaving her to wonder about his family's mental health history. When he didn't kiss her goodnight at the doors of Milbank Hall, she wasn't surprised.

Sarah had thrown a pillow at Catherine when she recapped the date. "You made him sit through the *asylum* movie? Oh God, Cat. What was that; some kind of test? What is wrong with you? Even *Abbot and Costello Meet Frankenstein* would have been better. At least then, you'd have an excuse to squeeze his arm and laugh about it."

"But I *did* clutch his arm over the tension." She threw the pillow back at Sarah.

Sarah shook her head in pity. "Tension isn't passion."

She'd thought at the time that Sarah was right. But when she stepped out the front doors this morning, still smiling from the note, and saw Peter leaning against a limestone column, she reconsidered that assessment. He was waiting for her; pairing his thumbnail with the pocketknife he carried everywhere, his shock of sandy hair stark against the snow-laden shrubs behind him. And before he looked up, she had time to muse that maybe the tension of learning she was out all night—though Sarah couldn't say where or with whom—had inspired enough passion to bring the farm boy straight to Milbank Hall bright and early on a cold day?

"Peter. What are you doing here?"

He folded his knife and dropped it in the front pocket of his trousers. She imagined his red scarf was probably knitted by his mother, and his knife likely bore an Eagle Scout insignia. There was nothing studied about the way he brandished it or lounged against that pillar. What *had* she been thinking taking him to see *The Snake Pit*?

"I just wanted to make sure you got home okay last night. Sarah said you were out late and she didn't think you'd been back since you went to the museum, so…I know it's none of my business, but the city's a dangerous place for a girl alone at night."

It was subtle, but the unspoken question hung in the arid air between them. *Was* she out alone? She was supposed to correct that concern of his by telling him whom she'd been with, and even though there was nothing amorous in her strange liaison with Hildebrand, she didn't have the first idea of how to explain their dealings and bristled at the notion that she should have to just because a country bumpkin suddenly felt possessive about her.

No, that wasn't fair. He was worried. It was writ plain on his face.

"That's sweet of you, Peter. But no need to worry. I'm fine, see? But I am late for class."

"Can I walk with you?"

"If you like."

Crossing the quad, Catherine noticed that Peter turned a few heads. Boys weren't entirely rare on the campus, but they did tend to stand out at the all girls school. She felt his body bump against her basket and looked up from the salted footpath just in time to see him tucking a brown paper bag in among her books. Flattened and fastened with tape, it looked like a parcel wrapped for mailing. He must have produced it from under his coat in an effort to pass it off to her discretely. She repositioned the basket handle on the crook of her elbow to accommodate the added weight and shot him a questioning look.

"The book you asked me to look for in the Butler Library."

A frisson of excitement quivered through her skin. "Not the von Junzt?"

Peter grinned guiltily. "Short term loan. I'm going to need it back by the end of the day tomorrow when they close for winter break."

"There are only four copies of *Unaussprechlichen Kulten* in public collections in the entire country. There's no way they let you check it out. Is this a prank to get my heart rate up? Am I going to find a copy of *Lady Chatterley's Lover* when I open it?"

He shook his head, all traces of humor and mischief gone from his face, and she realized what a great risk he had taken to please her. Peter

Philips, the straight arrow, had broken a rule that could get him in hot water for theft if he were caught. She'd been on the hunt for a copy of the book after noting a reference to it in her Man and the Supernatural textbook. Asking Peter to join in the search was something she'd done on a lark in the remote hope there might be a copy at Columbia. At best, she imagined angling for a quick look at the book in the confines of the Butler Library, where Barnard girls were barely tolerated. She'd never in her wildest dreams imagined he would abscond with it in a paper sack.

"How..."

"I make friends pretty much everywhere I go. They trust me because I keep my word. And I gave my word that this German abomination would be back on the shelf before anyone looks for it."

She knew she should take the package from the basket and thrust it back into his hands, urge him to return it right away, but the temptation was too great. If she passed up the opportunity, she might never have the chance to study the work again. According to Hildebrand, not even the Golden Bough had access to a copy. And if she didn't sleep tonight, she could transcribe the sections that interested her and get it back to him within the time he'd been granted by whoever was doing him the favor of looking the other way. She was a fast typist.

"Are you sure?"

"Course I am, or I wouldn't have brought it."

"Well, you really shouldn't risk it on my account. But I won't lie; it will be an enormous help in my studies. Barnard has come a long way since the days when they only had two shelves of books for the girls. Still, we can only dream of the resources you have at Columbia. Just promise me you'll be careful when you return it. It's a rare treasure. So are you." She squeezed his hand.

Peter smiled and looked away and she thought the rose bloom on his cheek wasn't from the December air. But when he turned to look at her again, his expression was serious. "Maybe you're the one who should be careful, Cat." He spoke quietly, though they were alone on the path now, approaching the ivy-covered brick arch where she would have to leave him behind for her lecture. She climbed a step and turned to face him at eye level, the basket swinging at her side. "What should I be careful of? Strange men tempting me with illicit reading materials?"

He laughed, but the sound had little humor in it. "I don't know much about that book, but my friend said it has a reputation. Do you know what happened to the author?"

She nodded.

"So then you know he was found murdered in a room locked from the inside?" Peter asked.

"Sounds like a case for Sherlock Holmes, right? Legends sprout up like mushrooms around books of this sort."

"What sort is that? Books about devil worshippers?"

Catherine sighed. "I mistook you for a man of science, Dr. Philips."

"Well, I'm not a doctor yet, and you're right, I don't believe in devils in the literal sense. But what do you hope to get out of it, if you don't mind my asking?"

"Knowledge."

He nodded, his expression thoughtful. "You know that mural of Athena they have at the entrance to the Butler Library? Goddess of Wisdom?"

"I've seen it."

"They say she's fending off the green demons of chaos and malevolence with her shield."

"Is that right?"

"There's a difference between knowledge and wisdom, Catherine. You know that, right? Same tree, different fruit."

She smiled. Still waters ran deep. "I'll keep that in mind. And thank you, Peter. Really. It means the world to me. I'll return it safe and sound."

"I know you will. Would you like to see a movie this weekend?"

"I was afraid you'd never ask."

"How about *Abbot and Costello Meet Frankenstein*?"

"Perfect."

* * *

They would take many more walks together as winter turned to spring and spring to summer—through city streets, brightly lit exhibit halls, and the shaded paths of Central Park. Peter would continue to loan Catherine rare books, usually in languages he couldn't read, and Catherine would show her appreciation while keeping the contents to herself. She never spoke of her initiation to him, and if one of her private sessions with Walter Hildebrand conflicted with a date, she would tell Peter she had a faculty consultation for a project. For the most part, these excuses felt like white lies. It was only her increasing discomfort with them that led her to the realization she had found something special. But by the time it fully dawned, other stars were aligned, and it was time for her to fly.

6

There was no mistaking the concrete castle. It towered over Esplanade Road, complete with Moorish arches, parapets, and stained glass windows, its gothic grandeur undermined only by its modern construction. Catherine found it on an afternoon hike up the shore from the beach shack she'd rented less than a mile to the south. It looked deserted in the daylight, the only visible human figure near the place was a mannequin perched at the side of the road, dressed in a tuxedo and holding a bucket emblazoned with the words, THE RESIDENT. Some joker's idea of a mailbox. The absence of a proper name on the bucket might have led her to wonder if Hildebrand had sent her to the right address. But it *was* the only castle on the street, and clearly the home of an eccentric. Satisfied she'd found it, she retreated to the beach house to meditate and fortify her psychic armor for the encounter ahead.

When she returned at dusk, the stained glass was backlit in hues of purple, green, and gold. The beach crowd had thinned with the end of the day, leaving only a lone surfer and a woman walking a dog along the path that cut through the bottom of the grassy embankment, which sloped down from the road. Cars passed at long intervals, their engines droning into the distance as they splashed their light up the coast. Catherine walked without a plan, dressed in sandals, clam digger pants, and a yellow blouse patterned with little red flowers that brought out the fiery hues in her hair. In a small leather pocketbook, she carried a Minox subminiature camera Hildebrand had loaned her, a model favored by spies for the covert capture of maps and documents during the war.

At his prior residence, a dilapidated mansion on Orange Grove in Pasadena, Parsons had opened his doors to all manner of fellow seekers. But following the revocation and reinstatement of his security clearance, Catherine worried that his habits might have changed. The government had scrutinized his associations going back decades. For all she knew, he could still be under surveillance, and if he thought he was, he might view a stranger with suspicion. She'd come armed with only a vague idea of the role she intended to play, thinking it best to feel out the situation and work with any opening that presented itself. After all, the Golden Bough had recruited her for her intuition and temerity. Or so they had said.

As she neared the castle, a percussive sound reached her ears—a rhythmic clattering, more spontaneous than music, echoing off the concrete edifice and chiming down over the road on the salty air. Looking up, she beheld an image out of a storybook: A pair of dark silhouettes, dueling with fencing foils on a stone patio set between the crenelated towers. Back and forth they danced, stabbing and parrying. *Clack! Clack-clack!* The thinner of the two men was faster, flailing and thrashing. He wore a red bandana over his head, reminding her of a pirate. His opponent, a tall man in a tweed vest and rolled-up shirt sleeves, fought more aggressively, but not without grace, grunting beneath a high shelf of curly black hair she immediately recognized from a newspaper photo Hildebrand had shown her during one of their sessions at the New York Public Library.

Jack Parsons.

The duel gave her an idea. She headed toward the water, searching the tide line for a piece of driftwood the length of a sword. It didn't take long to find a crooked stick that was white as bone. She carried it to the darkened sand from which the waves were retreating.

In an effort to internalize enough Starry Wisdom material to break the ice with her target, Catherine had transcribed a series of incantations and diagrams until they were etched into her memory. Now she drew one of these—the sigil of Lung Crawthok—in the damp sand, tracing the strange geometry from an angle that would render it recognizable from the deck of the castle. When it was complete, she drew a circle around the figure, careful to leave her footprints outside so that it shone flawless in the sunset as silver water seeped into the channels. She worked slowly, moving with meditative intent, and was surprised to find she was in a light trance by the time she finished.

The sigil complete, she knelt in the sand, closed her eyes, and waited, listening to the breath of the surf until she heard the gentle swish and crunch of shoes on the beach behind her.

"Who are you?"

A male voice, bemused. She looked up and saw him gilded by the sun, the castle a dusky lavender across the street behind him. The armpits of his white shirt were stained with perspiration around his tweed vest. The effect rendered him wild and well groomed all at once, his thin mustache neatly trimmed, his eyes fiery with curiosity. She nodded toward the castle where his sparring partner leaned on the iron patio railing, his fencing foil dangling idly from one hand.

"I dreamt of this place," she said. "That castle. I saw it in a dream before I ever saw it in the real world. And I somehow knew, when I woke, that it was a real place I would see on my trip." She smiled. "You must think I'm crazy, but it's true. Isn't that the strangest thing you've ever heard?"

The rocket scientist took a tentative step toward her. He bowed his knees, and lowered himself to the sand beside her. Gazing out at the ocean, he shrugged. "No, not really." He plucked her stick from out of the sand and brandished it at the sigil. "I'm familiar with this. Do you know what it is?"

"I saw that in my dream, too. If I've rendered it correctly."

"You have."

"What is it? I'm guessing a hieroglyph of some kind, but it's not from any culture I'm familiar with."

"Are you familiar with many?"

"I'm an anthropology student. It's what brings me to California. I'm checking out grad schools and making a short vacation of it. But that dream threw me off track. I knew I wouldn't be able to focus on anything else until I found the place." She tossed her head to let the wind unfurl her hair like a scarlet flag and cast her gaze up the coast. "Listen to me. I sound like a little girl, going on about castles and dreams and destiny. I'm really not like this. If you met me in ordinary circumstances, you'd know that. I'm actually quite rational when I'm not in California."

"Where are you from?"

"Massachusetts. Sorry, I never answered your first question." She extended her hand. "Catherine Littlefield."

"Jack Parsons." He threw the stick at the surf and shook her hand. "Where are you staying?"

Catherine tilted her chin south, toward Malaga Cove and the tree-lined bluff curving out into the ocean beyond. "I rented a small house on Torrance Beach. A shack, really. I had a feeling about the place, but I'm a little awestruck to find the castle so close to where I'm staying."

"It's my house."

She nodded. "I saw you and your friend fencing." Catherine waved at the man on the patio. He flicked the ash off a cigarette and returned the gesture, but she couldn't read his face in the fading light. "Is swordplay a requirement for living in a castle?"

Jack laughed. "Maybe it should be. I've been fencing since I was a kid. It's good for blowing off steam, but I can't always find a good partner. Kamen is Iraqi. We met at the college where I used to have a lab. Fortunately for me, fencing has caught on pretty much everywhere the Brits have planted their tents."

Catherine stood and brushed the sand from her bottom. She stepped out of her sandals and walked around the giant symbol, relishing the texture of the wet sand between her toes. It reminded her of home, of Salisbury Beach and Plum Island on the other side of the continent. Her parents hadn't understood why she needed to go to California. Ultimately, the fact that someone from a museum was funding the trip had been the best evidence she could offer that it was an important opportunity for her education. Her lessons with Hildebrand had filled in some curious gaps in her reading, but she suspected that here, on this dark stretch of beach, her true education was beginning. "I have to admit," she said, "this symbol gives me an uneasy feeling. In my dream, it wasn't encircled, but when I drew it, I felt it should be. To contain it, so it can't get loose. Is that crazy?"

"Not at all. You have good instincts for magic."

She met his eyes. "Is that what this is? It does resemble some symbols I've come across in my reading. Cornelius Agrippa comes to mind."

A muscle in his jaw twitched at the reference.

"Where do *you* know it from?" she asked.

He got to his feet and turned to the road, waving her along. "Come on. I'll show you."

Catherine hesitated. The channels she'd carved in the sand were drying out as the waves retreated from the beach. "I wish the tide were coming in to wash it away." This wasn't part of her act; she truly did.

Jack was halfway up the embankment when he spoke over his shoulder. "Give it time," he said. "In time, it will wash over everything."

She followed him through the tall grass, up the slope, and across the street to the waiting castle.

* * *

Jack placed the gramophone needle down on a record, setting serpentine strains of a violin to prowl the great room, slithering around the dark wood furniture and coiling in the corners. "Prokofiev," he said, uncorking a bottle of red wine and pouring generous measures into a pair of crystal goblets. "His Second Violin Concerto. I wore out my last copy while performing a daily invocation a few years back." He passed her a glass and made a toast. "To visionary dreams."

Catherine took in her surroundings: leather couches, Persian rugs, and wooden tables delineated the rooms of an open floor plan beneath an electric chandelier that threw shards of light across the scattered papers on a cluttered desk. The bookshelf nearest the gramophone was stocked with an eclectic assortment of chemistry and physics texts among the poetry and occult titles. Parsons took note of her interest in the spines and pointed a finger at one. "The von Junzt is where I've encountered the symbol you drew in the sand. And you mentioned Agrippa earlier. That tells me you're not a typical anthropology student."

"I've done a little research into the occult."

"Research." He tasted the word and found it lacking. "What about experimentation?"

Catherine sipped the wine. A pinot noir with cherry and chocolate notes. "Oh no, not for me. I need to maintain objectivity, after all." She looked from the bookshelf to another set of shelves where jars of powders and solutions loomed over a stained worktable. "Are you a scientist?"

Jack nodded. "My specialization is rocketry. Propellants...explosives. These days I design chemical plants. It's boring as hell compared to blowing things up and aiming for the stars. But now I'm closer to Hollywood, I've picked up some side jobs doing special effects."

"Rocketry! That sounds exciting."

"I got into it from a burning desire to put a man on the moon. Sadly, Uncle Sam only cares about how I can help him launch heavy bombers from short runways. So I've shifted my focus back to my *real* work."

"Which is?"

"Exploring *inner* space."

"How do you mean?"

He leaned against the arm of a sofa. "Well, I used to think we were most likely to encounter alien intelligence *out there*, among the stars. But my occult studies have convinced me we may not need rocket fuel at all. There are preternatural entities among us already, if we can only open our perception to commune with them. There could even be one in this room with us right now, hidden between the atoms in the air between us, visible along another plane, waiting for us to invite it in."

Catherine was well read on the concept of evocation, but the way he described it sent a chill down her spine, and she reappraised the room, half expecting to detect a shifting of shadows, a hint that they weren't alone.

A beaded curtain rustled, and she started. It was the man she'd seen on the roof, no longer wearing his bandana. "Food's ready, Jack. There's enough for three. Are you going to introduce me to your lady friend?"

"Catherine, this is Kamen Abdelmalek. He's a grad student in Mathematics at Cal Tech. He's also a better chef than I am, so you should stay for dinner." To Abdelmalek, he said, "Catherine is an Anthropology major at..."

"Barnard. In New York."

"She's visiting UCLA. As it happens, she shares our esoteric interests."

"Well in that case, you must dine with us. Do you like shepherd's pie?"

"I'd love to join, if it's really no trouble. The food smells delightful and I'm ravenous from walking the beach all day."

"Wonderful." Jack poured a third glass of the pinot and passed it to Abdelmalek. Together, the men were a stranger pairing than Catherine could tell watching them duel. Parsons had to be six-foot-two, radiant with confident charm, while his companion was short and stout with a shiny black beard and prematurely thinning hair framing a dusky complexion. His face seemed suspicious by default. His clothing was simple—blue slacks and a tan shirt with a high collar, like that of a priest. He took a sip of wine, then placed the goblet down on the long table and set to gathering the loose papers that littered its surface, tucking them into a manila folder.

"That's not necessary, Kamen," Jack said. "We can eat at the kitchen table."

"You two go on and get started. I'm just tidying up."

Catherine glimpsed sketches among the pages—bold lines of black ink depicting alien anatomy. But the drawings disappeared before the other papers, leaving her squinting at diagrams and hieroglyphs as Jack led her away with a gentle hand on her elbow. She gestured at the other cluttered surface in the room, the workbench. It was strewn with small mounds of powders and resins among vials of chemical solutions and charcoal briquettes. "Do you work on your explosives in the living room, Jack? Doesn't it put your books and papers in jeopardy, if not life and limb?"

Parsons laughed. "I won't lie to you and say I've never mixed anything volatile where I sleep, but no. These days, I keep that stuff in a shed. He waved her over to the bench and picked up a square of folded paper that held a reddish powder in the crease. He lifted it to her chin and said, "Smell. It's perfectly safe."

She closed her eyes and sniffed the air. The aroma was like nothing she'd ever encountered before: rich loam and dark musk with overtones of honey and brine.

"It's oddly intoxicating. What is it?"

"I'm manufacturing my own blends of incense, fine tuned to attract the entities we hope to entice across the membrane that separates our world from theirs."

"Careful, Jack," Abdelmalek said. The chaos of papers that had covered the table was now reduced to three neat stacks. The folder in which he'd gathered the artwork was nowhere in sight. "You'll scare her off."

"I told you, she's one of us. Led here by a dream."

"Let's hear all about it over dinner," Abdelmalek said, gesturing with his wine glass to whatever lay beyond the beaded curtain.

* * *

"This is really good." Catherine didn't know what kind of chemistry her host was dabbling in at his workbench, but the alchemy of food and wine was working to relax her. Her calves ached from hiking in the sand all day, but the tension she'd carried in her shoulders while navigating her improvised chance encounter with Jack was melting away. She reminded herself to be careful with alcohol and to guard against slipping on some aspect of her cover story. She'd intentionally hewn close to the facts of her life with only small embellishments and omissions to make this easier. Except, of course, for the very large omission that a secret society had tasked her with breaching the castle to report back on the doings of the magician she was dining with. She felt a grin spreading across her face as she thought of it, a completely absurd turn of events in her fledgling academic life. And it was falling into place. This morning, she'd set out from the beach house with no idea how to approach the task. Now, here she was, chatting with Parsons, who seemed perfectly willing to talk openly about magic with anyone who showed an affinity for it.

"You look amused," Abdelmalek said.

Catherine scooped up another spoonful of the mashed potato topping of the pie. "It's just delightful. Thank you for having me."

"You should stay the night," Jack said. "A girl shouldn't be walking the beach alone after dark."

"Oh, I couldn't. I don't have anything with me. And I wouldn't dream of imposing."

"Don't be silly. I have more rooms than I can use. And whatever you need for a single night, I'm sure we can dig up. Candy, my wife, left plenty behind when she took off to Mexico. I'm sure her clothes would fit you."

"Or I could escort you back to your rental," Abdelmalek offered.

"That's very kind. Both of you. I can feel the day catching up with me. Are you sure I wouldn't be putting you out if I took you up on the offer of a spare bed?"

"Of course not. It's settled then."

Abdelmalek gave Parsons a hard look, but Catherine was unsure of what passed between them. It was obvious the Iraqi mathematician didn't trust her. Beneath the veneer of hospitality, there was an undercurrent of hostility. But it wasn't his house, was it?

His eyes flicked from Jack's to hers and, sensing an impending interrogation, she decided to turn the tables. "So tell me about yourself, Kamen. How long have you been at Cal Tech?"

"I've just finished my first year."

"We're hoping they'll grant him another, to at least finish his Masters," Jack said, twisting a corkscrew into a second bottle of wine. Catherine resolved to refuse a refill.

"Why wouldn't they?"

"I had always hoped to study in America eventually, but the aftermath of the uprising in my country forced my hand in January."

"I'm afraid I have to plead ignorance," Catherine said. "With my studies, I don't get to read much international news."

"He's talking about the Al-Wathbah uprising," Jack interjected. "Kamen is too modest to take credit for his bravery, but he was among the student protestors when the police gunned down three-hundred of them in the street."

"More than that."

"I'm so sorry. That's absolutely horrific. But why wouldn't you be allowed to stay in America? You're a student. A political refugee as well, it sounds like."

Abdelmalek focused on his wine glass with a sardonic grin. "We were protesting the renewal of the Anglo-Iraqi Treaty, a document drafted to keep us under British control through a puppet monarchy. One would think that, of all nations, the United States would be sympathetic to our plight, but it is not that simple in the post-war world."

"The protestors were supported by the communist party," Jack said. "I don't know how it is at your school in New York, but the way things are going out here lately, that can cost you your job or student visa. Hell, they revoked *my* security clearance for a while just because I might have talked to a commie at a party one time."

"I've seen things in the paper, but I had no idea it was that bad. I have to admit I know more about Polynesian tribal politics than current events."

Jack lit a cigarette. "*All* politics are tribal. That's why we need people to look to the stars. To remember that we're all in it together on this rock. We need a *spiritual* revolution. But mark my words: When we do find proof of alien life, the first thing our leaders will ask is, 'How do we kill it?'"

7

Catherine lay awake in bed, listening to the ocean. The tide was high again, she could tell from the sound of the waves, their rhythmic white noise threatening to lull her to sleep. Parsons and Abdelmalek had stayed up late, smoking and finishing the second bottle, when she used her fatigue as an excuse to turn in early. She was genuinely exhausted, but also hadn't wanted to give Jack an opportunity to hit on her after his friend retired. She'd learned that Abdelmalek was lodging at the concrete castle for the remainder of the summer; a fact that Hildebrand's sources hadn't been aware of but that Catherine hoped might work to her advantage.

While Jack had been disarmingly open about his occult interests, she knew the Iraqi was more cautious. She thought if they were going to argue about the risk she posed to their privacy, they would do it now, at the first opportunity, while she was presumed to be sleeping. Her room was situated on the second floor along a balcony overlooking the great room where the men smoked and talked. But Jack kept flipping the record on the gramophone, masking their hushed conversation. Only once did the sharp edge in Abdelmalek's voice cut through the cloak of music, but his cursing in Arabic revealed nothing of value. Shortly after the outburst, he'd climbed the stairs and disappeared into what she assumed was his own bedroom at the far end of the balcony.

She swept the bed sheet aside and went to the window overlooking the street. The beach was too dark to see in detail, though the white breakers glowed in the light of a partial moon. She imagined the sigil she'd drawn must be washed away by now. She crept to the door, opened it, and gazed across the open balcony at Abdelmalek's door. No light shone through the cracks, but that didn't mean he was asleep. Jack's music continued below, a softer selection for the late hour. Eventually, a solo cello was joined by percussive sounds that didn't belong to the record. He was building a fire in the grate to warm the damp, drafty house.

Staying awake had been a struggle, jet lagged and coming off a day of exertion and intrigue. Now, hovering in the arched doorway, listening to the sounds from the room below, she felt her eyelids drooping, and realized she had no idea what sort of hours Jack kept. The hypnotic music seemed designed to lull her into a trance. She pinched her own earlobe, digging her fingernail into the soft flesh in an effort to remain alert. If she could outlast Jack, she might use her free-range access to the house to explore his papers and bookshelves. She knew her chances of finding the *Mortiferum Indicium* out in the open were slim, but she was determined to at least look for it on what might be her only night in the house.

There was a knock at the front door—the sharp rap of the lion's head knocker—setting her heart rate galloping in an adrenaline-washed instant. The bedroom had no clock, but judging by the tide, it had to be well after midnight.

Knowing that Jack would have his back turned to the balcony while opening the door, Catherine crept across the gallery and ducked behind a potted palm whose tall stalks and flat leaves obscured most of a small alcove where the balcony railing continued beyond the other bedroom. From her new vantage, she could see the stone fireplace between the matching leather couches below, a small blaze of driftwood crackling and casting its wavering light around the otherwise darkened room.

Jack ushered a woman in a polka dot dress into the room, kissing her on the cheek and removing a shawl from her shoulders. Her dark hair was sculpted back from her forehead in a long wave spilling down her back. Even in the dim light, her makeup telegraphed her high eyebrows and full lips across the room, like a child's drawing of a woman. Jack led her to one of the couches, where she sat and crossed her legs while he poured her a few fingers of pale green liquor from a decanter. She took the glass from him and sipped it. Without a word between them, Jack unbuttoned his shirt and set about preparing the room with the practiced motions of a man engaged in, if not a ritual, a task performed often. He knelt and rolled up the rug in the center of the room to reveal a symbol painted on the floor: A large triangle bounded by a circle, the angles marked with words she couldn't read, though the alphabet might have been Phoenician.

Jack surrounded the diagram with red candles and set a record of an Afro-Cuban drumbeat spinning on the gramophone. Then—following a quick stop at the workbench—he knelt by the fireplace. In a moment, streams of rich, white smoke flowed from a brazier on the hearth to pool across the floor like dry ice vapor, spicing the air with cinnamon, musk, and a metallic tang.

When Catherine noticed the woman again, she had risen from the couch and shed her dress. She handed something to Jack—her lipstick? He twisted the canister and used it to draw three sigils: one on her forehead, one between her breasts, and one on her navel.

The woman turned away from him, her gaze glancing along the balcony railing, and Catherine froze in place, relying on the tangle of shadows thrown by the palm leaves to conceal her. Jack undressed and lay on the wood floor in the center of the triangle, while the woman drained the glass of absinthe down her throat and set it on an end table.

Jack looked like a man lying in a shallow riverbed, the smoke pouring over him, obscuring his features. His companion knelt in the white stream, straddling him as he began to chant: *A ka dua tufir biu.*

The woman's spine undulated with the rhythm of their sex and her voice joined the chant.

The melody, simple at first, gradually modulated and ascended, coiling around the primal drum beat and curling upward in thorns of sound as the syllables changed: *Babalon-bal-bin-abaft…*

The door beside Catherine's perch on the balcony creaked open, and Abdelmalek stepped out, wearing a white silk robe. Catherine shrunk back into the dark corner behind the plant and watched him descend the stairs, his voice rising to join the chant. The woman riding Jack showed no sign of surprise at the sound of a third voice joining the litany. Her rhythm continued unbroken as the second man approached. Upon reaching the couple, Abdelmalek stood silhouetted in front of the fire and let his robe fall to the floor. His voice rose above the others, and the chant changed again: *Ia! Ia! Shabbathani Cyclothai... Ia! Ia! Shabbathani Cyclothai...Cyclothani, Cyclothani...Lung! Lung! Shabathani!*

The woman arched her back and brought her hands above her head, her palms together in a gesture of prayer. Her voice was a core of molten copper at the center of the chant. The voices of the men twined around it forming a frayed sheath that supported but never masked its brilliance. Tendrils of smoke spiraled around her torso and bloomed outward, assuming the shapes of a maelstrom of writhing eels, their howling mouths ringed with sharp wisps of smoke, leaving trails of vapor in their wake as they dove and snapped at the air. A crown of spikes coalesced around her head, carved from the same congealing smoke, a bouquet of white hooks blooming down her spine.

Abdelmalek mounted her from behind, straddling Jack's calves. The vapor hooks broke against his bare chest, reforming with each thrust of the woman's hips. He reached through the cyclone of eels and caressed her spiked breasts, then hunched forward and kissed her where sweat and smoke pooled around her collarbone.

The delirium of scents gathered in the thick air was shot through with the musk of sex, and Catherine felt her body responding to it, her growing horror laced with faint desire. The chant droned on incessantly, the syllables drilled into her mind. For a fleeting moment, she fought the impulse to blend her voice with the others and descend the stairs as Abdelmalek had until their trinity unfolded to take her in.

Then she swallowed, blinked, and rose from her stiff crouch behind the potted palm to slip through the arched doorway into Abdelmalek's darkened room.

8

LeBlanc had half a page left in the chapter he was reading when Whittaker tapped his shoulder with a hand like a T-bone steak, prompting him to look up from his paperback. The big man jutted his chin toward the street. "They have another visitor," he said, shaking a fresh toothpick out of the little box he kept in his shirt pocket and positioning it just so between his teeth, a sure indicator that he was ready to move. LeBlanc had given up on the prospect of any fresh action at the Parsonage—his partner's name for the concrete castle—over an hour ago. The appearance on the scene of the redhead at sunset was cause for some speculation, but that had exhausted itself by the time they'd finished their takeout burgers.

Less than a week into their assignment, LeBlanc and Whittaker had reached a mutual understanding that they were not compatible for small talk. Whittaker didn't seem offended that LeBlanc kept his nose in a book to pass the time they spent in the car, and Leblanc did his best to ignore the sounds of the game on the radio and the peppermint candies his partner crunched between his molars when he wasn't sucking on toothpicks. He almost wished the guy hadn't quit smoking. At least smoke was silent. But LeBlanc had to admit he admired the effort, even if it was inspired by the unrealistic fantasy that they were going to find themselves in a long distance foot chase or a fistfight. They carried guns to avoid both possibilities. And anyway, their suspects were hedonists, not athletes.

The first thing the agents had read in Parsons' file was a poem from the *Oriflamme,* a journal he'd published to promote the occult order he belonged to until 1946.

I height Don Quixote, I live on Peyote marihuana, morphine and cocaine.
I never knew sadness but only a madness that burns at the heart and the brain,
I see each charwoman ecstatic, inhuman, angelic, demonic, divine,
Each wagon a dragon, each beer mug a flagon that brims with ambrosial wine....

The mad scientist might have stamina in the bedroom, but he seemed unlikely to give them a run for their money in the course of surveillance. LeBlanc craned his head to look past Whittaker. They were parked on the corner of Avenue D, pointed toward the beach. The second woman of the evening had exited a taxi on Esplanade shortly after midnight and climbed the stairs to the front door of the castle, less than twenty yards to the south of their stakeout. "Was that Madeline?"

"No. Madeline has better tits. Pretty sure this is Salome. I can tell by the hair."

"The one who wouldn't talk."

"Right. Did you check out her affiliations?"

LeBlanc flipped his note pad open out of habit, even though he didn't need to read from it. Exceptions had a way of sticking in the memory. He flipped it closed again and swatted it against his paperback. "She was only picked up for hooking once, and that was years ago, when she first came to America. Clean record ever since."

"So she's visiting Jack for love, not money?"

"Love or faith."

"Spell it out, will ya? What is she OTO?"

LeBlanc shook his head. Whittaker hoisted an eyebrow. "Starry Wisdom?"

"Yeah. Long Beach congregation."

Whittaker whistled around his toothpick. "So a different congregation than Abdelmalek. What do you make of that?"

LeBlanc shrugged. "Maybe nothing. It *is* a lot closer."

"Or? You sound like there's an *or.*"

"Or maybe Abdelmalek doesn't want word to get around his own congregation that he's doing rituals with Parsons."

"Gotta be a tight knit community, even with the distance. I mean, they got phones, right? How many Starry Wisdom churches are there in America?"

"Not many, and most are in Rhode Island or Massachusetts. But you know California. If it's a weird church, we've got at least two."

Whittaker chuckled and opened the driver's side door.

"Where you going, chief?"

"Where are *we* going. C'mon. Time to play peeping Tom and Jerry."

"Really?"

"You're not getting paid to read. What the hell is that anyway? It's not even in English."

"*The Stranger*. It's a novel. Camus."

"Gesundheit."

They approached the castle from the north. The only exterior lights were on the east and west sides of the building, mostly spillage from the elevated patios. Crouching low and stepping lightly, they blended into the shadows along the fence line. Neither man carried a flashlight. They weren't police, and if anyone (including the police) pressed them on their business, they would have to fall back on fake private investigator credentials or try and buy time by insinuating they were FBI without flashing badges. The irony was that they *were* federal agents, but the agency they worked for wasn't supposed to exist, and admitting it did would land them in more hot water than a charge for impersonating law enforcement. Even as agents of SPEAR, they didn't know what the acronym stood for. Their paychecks came from the Department of the Interior. LeBlanc's best guess was Special Physics Exploration And Research. Whittaker's favorite was Shit Pay And Early Retirement, though LeBlanc didn't care enough to point out that he had the vowels reversed. One thing they agreed on was that if the agency was ever in danger of exposure by documents or gadgets in their possession, their exit strategy was to Sucker Punch Everyone And Run.

The darkened ground on the side of the castle proved mercifully clear of obstacles, but they took it slow, aware that a single piece of debris clattering away from a misplaced foot would be enough to send them scurrying back to the car. Jack's midnight visitor had been inside for some time when they reached a stained glass window that pulsed with the uneven light of candle flames or a fireplace within. Whittaker laced his fingers together and squatted to give LeBlanc a leg up. LeBlanc's first instinct was to reject the idea, but he didn't have a reason his partner would accept, just an aversion to the indignity of climbing the other man only to scuff his hands on the concrete wall and rusty window frame for maybe a quick glimpse of a midnight tryst from a bad angle. He sighed and stepped onto the human escalator. At least Whittaker knew better than to propose that they do this the other way around, much as he probably would have preferred to be the eyes of the operation.

The big man was a stable lift. LeBlanc only wobbled for a single precarious second, and that was owing to his own reluctance to lock his knee and put his full weight down on his partner's hands. When he committed to the act, he found himself rising smoothly to the height of the arched window. The stained glass depicted yellow flowers against a purple sky, the yellow pale enough that he could discern the basic contours of the room through it. Parsons, visible from the chest up, was undressing. The furniture, floor, and anyone seated were too low to see from this vantage.

"Can you go any higher?"

With a heave and a grunt from below, LeBlanc gained a few more inches. He scrabbled for purchase on the rusty iron window ledge to take some of his own weight, knowing that even his relatively light body would only feel heavier to the other man the higher he had to lift it. But there was nothing he could get a firm grip on, and not enough of the yellow glass to see more than the top of Jack's bare ass floating in coils of smoke.

"Anything?"

"Yeah, they're gonna screw. Big surprise."

With a grunt, Whittaker brought him back down and tipped him onto the weedy ground with what felt like an intentional lack of grace.

"What about the other two? The Arab and the redhead. You see them?"

LeBlanc caught the concrete wall with the flat of his hand to keep from tumbling into it. "No. Just Parsons. Naked already. But for all I could see, they might be having an orgy in there with Howard Hughes and all the neighbors. It's a bad angle. I just got lucky Jack was in front of it."

Whittaker shifted from one foot to the other, like a cat thinking of jumping for the window ledge. "What do we do? Pick her up for questioning when she leaves?"

"No. She's loyal to the cause. We'd get nothing out of her and she'd tell them straight away. Come on. Let's hop the gate and try the patio."

Their prospects from the raised patio weren't much improved. The big oak door to the second floor interior was locked. Two windows peered out the west-facing wall on either side of the patio overlooking the beach. These were functional casement types, not stained glass, but they were too high, too far out of reach, and too dark to suggest that they might provide a view of the inhabitants. LeBlanc sized them up for a moment. When he turned around, Whittaker had disappeared. It took him a moment to spot the man's bulk, flat against the castle wall, edging around the side of the building toward another stained window on the south side, with only a thin ledge a few inches wide to support the toes of his Oxfords.

LeBlanc risked a stage whisper. *"What the hell are you doing?"*

A piece of the ledge crumbled away in a shower of concrete dust and Whittaker's right leg swung out wide behind him before circling back around and finding a firmer footing a little farther on.

"Frank! Get back here."

But Whittaker had reached the window, his hands gripping the metal frame, his face so close to the glass that he had to be fogging it with his breath. LeBlanc couldn't tell what this window depicted, but even if it was the same flower pattern he'd peered through on the ground floor, Whittaker was higher up on this one and had more options. He must have seen something because he was staring with one eye squeezed shut, like a pervert at a peep show.

LeBlanc gave up on coaxing him back and decided to make himself useful as a lookout. He walked a circuit around the patio, scanning the street for neighbors and passers by who might notice the big man clinging to the gray façade and alert the authorities. For the time being, the street and beach were both deserted. He sighed with relief. The last thing they needed was a cop on the neighborhood beat throwing a light on them.

As if conjured by the thought, a light flared up in one of the bedrooms above, dimming quickly like a match after the head is spent. Frozen in place, LeBlanc stared at the window, waiting for a face to appear. When none did, he hurried around the corner to the railing Whittaker had climbed to reach the ledge. The big guy was pressing his ear to the glass now, eyes closed, straining to hear something.

Leblanc could hear it too: a droning chant. The words eluded him. *"Frank."*

Whittaker opened his eyes.

"Come on. We have to get out of here. Someone's upstairs." He gestured with a circular wave. This time, his partner seemed to comprehend the urgency. Whittaker could move quickly when he needed to, even on his tiptoes. In less than a minute, he was jumping down onto the patio from the railing.

LeBlanc hurried him, jabbing a finger toward the illuminated window.

"Gotta be the redhead," Whittaker said. "She's the only one missing from the festivities in there."

LeBlanc ducked his head between his shoulders and hurried to the concrete stairs they'd taken from the street. He'd descended the first ten before sensing that Whittaker wasn't following, then bounded silently back up to find the man stock still at the edge of the patio, staring out at the ocean with the same intensity he'd previously focused through the stained glass. No, this was different. That had been lurid fascination. This, to the extent that Whittaker's doughy features could convey it, was awe.

LeBlanc followed his gaze.

Something glowed under the water, a phosphorescent sigil wavering in the shallows.

Whittaker glanced down at him. "Shoulda brought the binocs. I left them in the glove box. You're eyes are better than mine. Can you tell which symbol that is?"

LeBlanc couldn't be sure without a closer look. He shook his head. "Let's check it out. He shot a last look at the window beyond his partner's towering silhouette. The candlelight still danced beyond the glass, but there was no one looking back.

* * *

Catherine closed the door enough for it to stick in the swollen wood of the frame. A concrete house on the beach had to be one of the dampest places a man could choose to live, but she was grateful the tight fit didn't require her to latch it, allowing for a quieter retreat to her own room if the chanting stopped. For now, the sound was her only assurance that she wouldn't be walked in on while searching the room. It droned through the house, tinged with harmonics that set the crystal chandeliers chiming. The melody was primitive, but the layering of voices complex; a triad of overtones as exotic as the incense that rose to the balcony on the house's drafty currents, trailing her into the darkened room.

She relied on the scant light from the window to locate a candlestick on the bedside table, and lit it from a matchbook she found on the same table, snuffing the match between her thumb and forefinger before tucking it into her pocket to avoid leaving evidence of her presence behind. The room bloomed into visibility, stark and empty except for a suitcase and a few hanging shirts in the closet and a briefcase on a desk beneath the window. Would the smell of burning wax linger in the air? She hoped the incense from below would mask it.

The briefcase, a scuffed and worn thing that had probably started its life in a shop in Baghdad, wasn't locked. She sprung the latches and lifted the lid carefully, propping it against the wall. Inside, she found a stack of papers, a pad of graph paper covered in calculations and strange runes, and what might have been a weapon or tool of some kind—a silver spike about nine inches long with an ornately carved handle. She couldn't discern what the carving was meant to depict, but thought it might be some kind of dragon. Was this a ritual dagger? If so, why hadn't Abdelmalek brought it downstairs with him to the ritual?

Maybe he has the only tool he needs for that.

She knew that daggers were most often used for banishing, and tonight, the trio seemed to be engaged in an invocation; the summoning of some force the woman was lending her body to.

B.
C or K.
G.
D.
F.
A.
L.
P.
Q.
N.
X.
O.
E.
M.
J.
Y.
I.
H.
R.
Z.
U, V, W.
S.
T.

The papers appeared to be mimeograph copies of a handwritten manuscript, but the alphabet was alien to her. Scattered amid the copies were a few pages of original parchment. Of these, some were covered almost entirely in splotches of what looked like spilled India ink. Drawings of marine creatures adorned the margins, as unrecognizable as the words and letters—unnerving specimens, bug eyed and bedecked with rows of teeth and claws. If such things existed in nature, they likely roamed beyond the reach of the sun's longest rays.

She'd waited out most of the night in bed fully clothed, even though Jack had provided her with a selection of nightgowns to choose from. Now she took the subminiature spy camera from the front pocket of the pants she'd spent the day hiking in. She slid it open, her pulse galloping and her hands clammy. Documenting everything was a task too big to complete in the scant time that might be available to her. She flipped through the chaos of papers, searching for anything that might be significant and complete enough to warrant a photo.

When she found what she was looking for, the shock of it took a moment to absorb, and she realized that despite acting on Hildebrand's instructions, she had never really expected to find what he'd sent her here for. Sure, Jack was into some strange cult activity, strange enough even to conjure an entity to near visible appearance with the aid of a medium and some concoction of apparently sentient smoke. But the notion that an ancient artifact was concealed in Cleopatra's Needle in New York, and that a West Coast faction of the Starry Wisdom had kept records of it for generations because of the threat it posed to their apocalyptic plans…well, she wasn't going to turn down the promise of adventure just because the chances of finding proof were remote, but she'd also never doubted how remote they were.

And yet, here it was: Three pages of runes flowing around drawings of a scarab beetle clenching a gem in its pincers. Two of the pages were on parchment and appeared to contain verses or incantations. The other, rendered in the blue mimeograph ink, appeared to be a cypher key, with neat columns of runes and their English equivalents. If the parchment verses could be decoded using the English key, then she could be sure it didn't originate in ancient Egypt, though the simple fact that it was on parchment and not papyrus was enough to indicate that much. Still, that didn't mean it hadn't been passed down through generations of the latter day Starry Wisdom Church, which had left footprints in a scattering of Middle Eastern countries before jumping the Atlantic and emerging above ground in 1844.

Something thudded against the outside wall of the castle, causing Catherine to spill the papers across the floor and under the bed. She stared at the closed door. The chanting continued without interruption. She knelt and gathered the papers, thanking her guardian angel that she hadn't dropped them onto the candle and knocked it from its silver base.

When she'd gathered the bundle and set the two scarab pages on top, she realized that she had no idea what order the pages had been in before the spill. For a moment, she considered putting them back in the briefcase and searching for a window she could climb out of. All she'd told the men was that she was renting a shack down the beach. They couldn't knock on every door in the middle of the night. And if she left the briefcase where she'd found it, Abdelmalek might not even notice the missing pages until morning. But if she fled in the night, she would be burning a bridge behind her, admitting by her actions that she'd come on false pretenses. Fate had literally handed her the keys to the castle. She couldn't afford to squander the opportunity to learn more from Parsons just for the sake of a manuscript she could only hope to decipher a fragment of. Better to document what she could and take her chances prying for more in the morning. After all, these men had worked with the material. And judging by what she had seen from the balcony, they were getting results. What might they have learned that she could never hope to glean from writings alone? If they discovered that her curiosity extended to prowling, would they really harm her? She thought not. More likely, they would throw her out. So why leave before she had no choice in the matter? They didn't know her allegiances, and truth be told, neither did she. She was fumbling in the dark, grappling with the contours of a mystery that might ultimately align her with Jack's inscrutable aims. He had been so open and welcoming, had seen in her a kindred spirit. The least she could do was talk with him tomorrow about his nocturnal exploits. Given the volume of the chant reaching a crescendo mere feet below the bed they'd given her to sleep in, they were taking no pains to hide what they were up to.

How much longer could they go? The mantra rolled on with no hint of exhaustion. Catherine positioned the scarab pages in the candlelight and lined up the viewfinder. Between each click of the shutter, the camera trembled in her fingers.

* * *

"What is it?" Whittaker stood in the dry sand beyond the high tide line, his oxfords tangled in crabgrass and the wind-blown husks of dried seaweed. LeBlanc's shoes lay abandoned a few yards closer to the surf. For once, it was the big man hanging back while the thin man examined the threat. LeBlanc waded into the shallows, drawn to the manifestation by an irresistible fascination, his slacks rolled up over his knees.

A creature of light rose from the submerged sigil, breaking the surface of the water and towering over the waves. It had to be at least twelve feet tall, a transparent projection of violet light, though what medium the light used to hang in the air with three-dimensional solidity, LeBlanc couldn't say. There was no mist or fog on the air to sustain it. He recognized the form as Lung Crawthok, a humanoid deity with crustacean armor, a tail like that of a scorpion, and rows of claws curling from its ribs. The characteristic details were all there, as described in the church documents—the harpoon staff and fang-tipped flower petals of flesh framing the rictus of horse teeth. But nothing he had read could have prepared him for the experience of standing in its presence, even in the thin form of holographic light. The creature was almost beautiful, torso set low in a balanced, bent-legged-warrior stance, head slowly scanning the horizon. Its shimmering face radiated an alien nobility and savage intelligence, and he knew in his bones and balls that he stood in the presence of a nascent god.

The creature gave no indication that it was aware of him. Its cold eyes seemed to be focused on the castle, acknowledging something LeBlanc couldn't see, as if its gaze could penetrate the concrete walls in the same way that he could see the stars through its towering form.

He advanced through the gentle surf and reached out with a tentative hand. A sound of reproach escaped Whittaker's throat, carrying on the wind from the man's position up the beach, an inchoate groan. But

LeBlanc paid it no heed. He thought of the microbial life that shared the environment with mankind, the dust mites and other organisms that crowded the air and earth but failed to attract our regard. He was as insignificant to this creature as those life forms were to him. The scale was not as different, but the planes of existence they occupied were.

So what was facilitating this insubstantial perception? Was it the sigil carved in the sand? The ritual unfolding in the castle? Some combination of the two? Or was it the chant?

He passed his hand through the shaft of the creature's staff, prepared to turn and flee if the gesture awakened it to his presence. Nothing. Not even a hint of resistance in the air as his fingers traveled through the light. Not a flicker. They called this god the Lurker at the Threshold, the Guardian at the Gate. It was the consort of the goddess Shabbat Cycloth, and her protector. Hers was the name they chanted inside the castle.

A stone plunked into the water a few feet away, breaking the trance LeBlanc was falling into. He looked up the beach at Whittaker, who had come closer and was holding his discarded shoes, waving him back. Deciding that if the monster couldn't see him it probably couldn't hear him either, he called out, "Do you see it? Lung—" He stopped himself short of uttering the name, fearful that the sound might complete the manifestation. "The creature," he finished.

"Yeah," Whittaker said. "Come on. It's fading."

LeBlanc saw that he was right. The light was dissolving, the phosphorescent lines of the sigil dimming.

"They must be winding down," Whittaker said.

LeBlanc plodded out of the surf and Whittaker handed him his shoes. He took them absently, staring back at where the creature had been. Whittaker clapped a hand on his shoulder. "Snap out of it, Jeremy. Let's go. If she leaves, I want to tail the cab."

9

Catherine woke in a room almost white with sunlight. For a disorienting moment, she couldn't remember where she was, and then it all came back. Not a dream, but a long night of intrigue. The sound of the ocean reached her through the window, mingled with the cries of gulls and children, and she sat up, aware of two things at once: For the room to be this bright with a westward facing window, she must have slept very late. And if no one had disturbed her, it was likely that her late-night prowling had gone undetected.

She looked at the clothes Jack had left for her, folded and stacked on a chair. She'd left the nightgowns untouched, opting to sleep in half of the clothes she'd worn the previous day. Now she considered a fresh change and quickly decided against it, opting instead to shake out her own salt and sand crusted pants and wear them again. After taking the temperature of Jack's hospitality, she would maybe take a quick shower, but for now she didn't want to be beholden to him any more than was necessary. Nor did she want to remind him of his estranged wife. Most of all, she didn't want to complicate her exit if she found a need to make it quick.

Overnight, the castle house had felt dank and drafty, a cave of shadows. Now, in daylight, it had an entirely different personality: spacious, airy, bright, and inviting. The acrid aroma of incense had been cleared away by the morning breeze, replaced with the scents of coffee and grilled sausages beckoning from the open kitchen area below.

She found Jack at the long table, alone among his scattered papers, as if Abdelmalek had never made the effort to hide them from her prying eyes. A mug of black coffee sat neglected at his elbow, and a crust of toast dangled from his hand like he'd forgotten entirely that he was eating it. He looked surprised at the sight of her when she reached the bottom of the stairs, but with a quick smile, he bounced to his feet, tossing the unfinished toast onto a plate, and waving her toward a chair.

"Catherine. Good morning. Did you sleep okay? I know the bed is a little rickety."

"It was lovely. I must have needed the rest more than I realized." She scanned the walls for a clock. "What time is it?"

Jack glanced at his watch. "Half-past breakfast. But I've kept it warm for you. Sausages and coffee are on the stove. How do you like your eggs?"

She almost told him not to bother, but her stomach was already growling at the smell of food. "Scrambled? I can make them. I don't want to disturb your work."

"Nonsense. You're my guest. Please, sit down. Do you take cream, and sugar?"

"Just a little cream. Where's Kamen?"

"He took a drive down to Long Beach. I don't expect him back until later."

Catherine thought of the briefcase. She should have checked to see if the other bedroom door was ajar before coming downstairs. She could have peered in to see if the case remained where she'd left it. She let her eyes roam the papers scattered across the table. Were any of those she'd seen last night among them? These looked just as strange. The mimeographed cypher key jumped out at her. But for all she knew, this could be a second copy.

"What's in Long Beach? Sorry. I don't mean to pry…"

Behind her, Jack cracked an egg in to a pan and fired a burner. "His church has a chapter there. He's giving a friend a ride home. She dropped by after you retired. I hope our chanting didn't keep you up."

So there would be no effort to deny the events of the previous night. Perhaps he already knew that she had been through the papers in the briefcase and didn't care? She dropped any pretense of disinterest and openly studied the pages closest to her seat at the table. They were covered with visionary verses and bold pen-and-ink drawings depicting a grotesque bestiary of demigods.

And on the 31st of October 1948, BABALON called on me again, and I began the last work, that was the work of the wand. And I worked for 17 days, until BABALON called me in a dream, and instructed me on an astral working. Then I reconstructed the temple, and began the Black Pilgrimage, as She instructed.

And I went into the sunset with Her sign, and into the night past accursed and desolate places and cyclopean ruins, and so came at last to the City of Chorazin. And there a great tower of Black Basalt was raised, that was part of a castle whose further battlements reeled over the gulf of stars. And upon the tower was this sign

If there was a glyph or sigil that followed, it was obscured by another sheet of paper, tossed askew across the handwritten text. This was one of the drawings. It depicted a horned and hooded figure, four-armed like a Hindu god, its face concealed in shadows but for an eye like a shard of light. Its four hands played the strings of a strange instrument—a lute or guitar with a crescent shaped sound hole.

She drank in the details of the other images, her eyes flicking from one to the next, her hunger—ravenous just a moment ago—turning sour in her stomach. There were eyeless, long fingered creatures holding candles before their chittering teeth; a giant winged beast crouching over Moai idol heads howled at the sky, its head sprouting enough eyes, tentacles, and horns to defy earthly evolution; a diagram of the silver dagger she'd found in Abdelmalek's case, surrounded by more of the cypher runes she'd seen on the scarab pages; a smiling Negro wearing a crown and strange spectacles, surrounded by luminous marine creatures that reminded her of the eels she'd glimpsed from the balcony, swirling in the greasy smoke. The memory made her shiver.

Another fragment of writing caught her eye, a sliver of a page. Was this in Jack's hand?

I, BELARION, ANTICHRIST, in the year 1949 of the rule of the Black Brotherhood called Christianity, do make my Manifesto to all men.

He set a plate of eggs and sausage down beside her. She took a sip of the coffee, hoping it would clear her groggy head. She needed to clarify what was going on here. Had the incense fumes and jet lagged sleep deprivation caused her to hallucinate last night? To twist smoke and shadow into a shape like the one on this drawing of a demonic goddess enswathed in a skirt of eels? Or had she witnessed a manifestation of some kind?

"What are these, Jack? Did *you* draw them?"

He laughed, sat down, and scratched his scalp through the cascade of black curls that hung over his high brow. "No. I'm not good for anything but engineering diagrams. These are Candy's. She's a real artist, which is fortunate because without her, the only documentation we'd have would be my poetic ramblings."

"Documentation of what?"

"We did a working before she went away. Abdelmalek introduced us to the evocations. Ancient starry wisdom, he calls it. Now, I've tried all kinds of magic, had all kinds of revelations, but this was something else. He has a mirror we use to see the visions in. Pitch black obsidian. I would perform the ritual, and Marjorie—Candy—would draw what she saw in the glass. She's sensitive, a seer. Modern humans don't have the right kind of primordial vocal cords for the chants to fully manifest the old gods and goddesses, and Kamen says without those harmonics, we'll never bring them through all the way to our plane, but we could bring them close. Call them up to the surface of the black glass."

"Were you working with the mirror last night? I heard chanting. Could I see it?"

"Kamen wouldn't approve. His family is charged with protecting it, a duty he takes very seriously. For him to let us use it at all was...risky. He said he saw raw talent in us that's been rare among his congregation, so he let us experiment. Under his supervision only. Candy documented a whole pantheon before it got to be too much for her and she took off. First to Europe, then to Mexico."

"Who was your visitor last night? Another medium?"

"I guess you could say that. Are you gonna eat your eggs? Did they come out all right?"

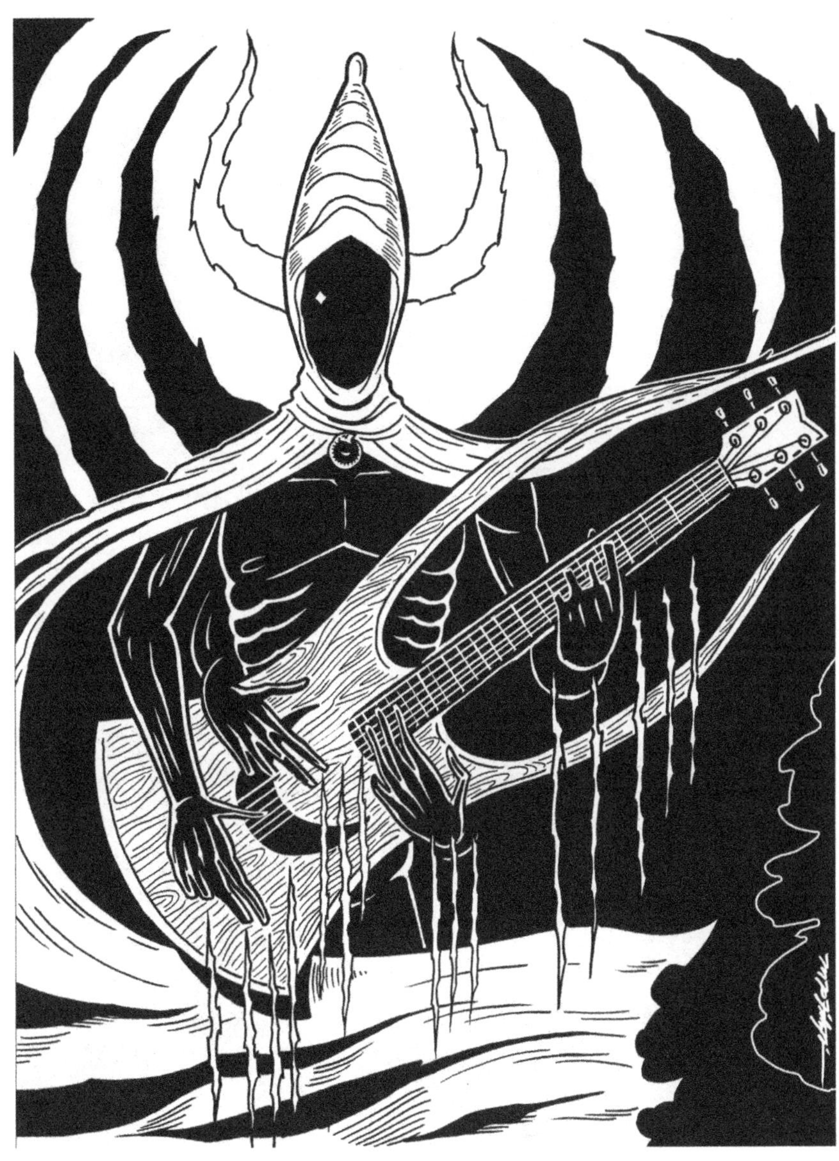

STARRY WISDOM CHURCH
B.
C or K.
G.
D.
F.
A.
E.
M.
I, Y, or J.
H.
L.
P.
Q.
N.
X.
O.
R.
Z.
U, V, W.
S.
T.
ORDER OF THE CRAWLING CHAOS

"Sorry. It's just fascinating stuff. The food is delicious." For a while, she ate in silence, studying the drawings. Then she wiped her hands on her napkin and touched the corner of a page. "This is a strange god. What's his name?" It was the black man in the crown and glasses.

Jack shook his head. "Not a god. Maybe a prophet? I don't know. That was a problem we ran into. Some of these are easy to identify from Abdelmalek's grimoires, but others were probably...prophetic glimpses of apocalyptic events in the future. That's the best theory we have so far, anyway. That's part of the problem of using a psychic and a mirror. You don't always get a pure evocation. She might see probabilities that the god is related to instead. Glimpses of the future or past."

"I'm not sure I understand."

He smiled. "I'm not so sure I do, either. It might even be a blessing in disguise that Candy left. We were relying too much on her vision. Now that we're using the incense instead of the mirror as a manifesting medium, the entities are possessing the physical body more, so it filters that other stuff out."

"These images are incredible. Horrible...but also...beautiful. You saw these things?"

"Only through Candy's eyes. I caught glimpses, but I'm not as sensitive." He searched Catherine's eyes. "I bet you'd see all kinds of things."

"Maybe you should test me. You said Kamen is in Long Beach? He'll probably be gone all day." She swept her fingertips over the papers, stirring them like an inky pool from which something might surface. Jack didn't seem to mind. He watched them roam. The eggs went cold. She plucked a sheet of verse. "What's all this about the Antichrist?"

"You're having breakfast with him."

She raised an eyebrow. "You're the son of the devil, Jack?"

"Maybe. My father's name was Marvel. It's my name, too. Marvel Whiteside Parsons. But my mother took to calling me John after she divorced him for running around on her. So that's my real dad. But when I was a boy, I tried to summon the devil."

"I don't believe in the devil."

"Then you aren't a Christian?"

"My parents are. Did he show up? The devil."

"If you don't believe in him, why would you ask that?"

"Because I do believe in the power of the mind."

"Did you see what we conjured last night?"

Catherine nodded.

"That was more than just the power of the mind. Wouldn't you say?" He lit a cigarette and waved it over the pile of sketches. "What did you see?"

Catherine tapped the drawing of the eel enswathed goddess. "This. In the smoke around the woman."

"Her name is Salome. She was channeling the goddess. Shabbat Cycloth."

"People can see what they want to see in smoke or clouds."

Jack leaned in. "Ah, but you didn't know what we were conjuring, did you? How would your subconscious mind know to make eels out of ribbons of smoke? It wouldn't, unless you know more about all of this than you're letting on. Do you? You came here and drew the sigil of the goddess' consort in the sand. What *do* you know, Catherine?"

She took the cigarette from him and drew a long drag off it, then exhaled the smoke at the ceiling, looking for something atavistic in the plume before it dissipated. "I'm just trying to understand my dreams. Are you trying to scare me away?"

"Why would I do that?"

She handed the cigarette back. "I don't know. What kind of guy tells a girl he's the Antichrist over breakfast? Are you trying to convince me you're evil?"

"Good and evil are for children. I have a dark side; we all do. What I'm against is the repression of that darkness, the oppression of sexuality and personal liberty. The hypocrisy of the Christian epoch. Science was supposed to save us from that slavery. It was supposed to empower us to reach for the stars." He scoffed. "Look where it's led us instead. More oppression. A bomb that can wipe out all life on the planet. Hitler and Stalin and their repressive regimes empowered by the iron fist of technology. And now? After the war? The best minds in America too afraid to dream. Too afraid to aspire to anything loftier than security. An age of fear. Well, it's coming to an end, and I am come to herald its demise. That's what my pilgrimage in the desert revealed to me. Soon

Babalon will be born, ushering in a new age. And through her sacred gate, the gods will spill forth into our world, and the oceans will be the amniotic fluid from which they rise to scream at the sky."

"Is that why you live on the beach? In a sand castle? Front row seat for the apocalypse?"

Jack laughed. It made him look boyish. "I'm starting to think maybe it is. When I bought the place, I thought I just needed a change of scenery after so many years in the desert. At the time, I hadn't even heard of the Great Old Ones. But you know how it is: your deep mind knows what you need. That's what brought *you* here."

Catherine took in the rooms around her for the first time in daylight. The house was dustier and more cluttered than she'd noticed at night. On the balcony, she spotted the potted palm she'd hidden behind. Did Abdelmalek tell Jack she'd rummaged through his briefcase? Did he even know?

"I'm not so sure about this dark side of yours, Jack. You welcomed me into your home, offered me a bed and a meal. And maybe you consider me a kindred spirit, but you've been very open about your interests, dark as *they* might seem to some. But I doubt that you have a dark heart."

He stubbed his cigarette out. "It's darker than you think, darling. Believe me."

"Convince me."

For the first time since she'd made his acquaintance, he seemed to consider his words carefully before speaking. But she didn't know if he was deliberating what to tell, or how to tell it.

"I cursed my father."

When she showed no reaction, he went on. "I don't mean I called him a no good son-of-a-bitch, I mean I *cursed* him, like put a hex on him."

"And did it work?"

"Hell yes. And the damnedest thing is that to this day I don't even know how I did it. It was that deep mind again, you know? Don't mistake me; I'm not blaming my subconscious. I must have meant to do it or it wouldn't have happened. But I didn't do a proper spell to make it happen."

"Tell me."

He ran a hand through his hair and expelled a sigh through pursed lips. Then he played with his pack of cigarettes, contemplated lighting another, and ended up tossing the pack aside. "My mother wouldn't let him see me when I was a kid, and then I guess he was traveling the world for some years. He was a marksman in the army. Chased Pancho Villa across Mexico, was stationed in the Philippines for a while. Even found time to have another family. Anyway, when I was at Cal Tech, working with the rocketry group, he shows up at my house with this half-brother of mine. Charles. Fourteen-year-old kid. I don't harbor any resentment toward him. I was with my first wife at the time. So…this man who was never there for me when I needed him shows up at my door and wants to get to know me. Strangest goddamn thing. So, of course, Helen asks him to stay for dinner, and I guess he could see how awkward it was for me because he declined. I don't even remember what we talked about. I showed him around my laboratory where I was working on the rocket engine prototypes, and eventually, he left with his boy. That was it.

"But what I learned years later is that shortly after that visit, he had a heart attack. The doctors told him he had twenty-four hours to live! But they were wrong. He lived another ten years after that, but he was never the same. He had to be committed to a mental hospital because he felt the shadow of death hanging over him for the rest of his life, always sure it was coming. He suffered a total breakdown—delusions, hallucinations about his soul leaking out of his chest. For ten years."

"That's terrible."

"I saw him one more time, when I was on a business trip to D.C. Visited him at St. Elizabeth's psychiatric hospital. He was a wreck of a man by then. I'm not sure he even knew me, but right after I saw him again, he died. It wasn't even his heart that got him in the end but meningitis. Weird, huh? I hadn't even started on a proper study of magic when he showed up at my house in Pasadena back in '36. But I know… I *know* something in me triggered that long chain of suffering and clapped it on him like a shackle. Something in my dark heart. Can you believe that?"

Catherine thought about it. His eyes were glassy and distant. She touched his hand on the table. "You know what I *can* believe, Jack?"

"What?"

"That when you called up the devil as a boy, you were looking for a father."

10

The Starry Wisdom chapter in Long Beach held their masses in a crumbling stucco building that had been a Pentecostal church until even the fringe branches of Christianity started losing congregants to the new religions sprouting up in the land of the eternal gold rush. Situated near the waterfront, the church could have been abandoned for all of the effort it made to identify the sect it served in 1949. The only sign to the faithful was a small iron emblem—a triangle in a circle—hanging from a nail where the shadow of an absent cross still stained the sunbaked facade.

Whittaker and LeBlanc had slept in shifts in the car, then trailed Kamenwati Abdelmalek's second-hand Hudson coupe when he left the castle with Salome shortly after daybreak. Abdelmalek had found time to shave, even if he'd slept less than the pair of agents assigned to him. He carried his familiar black briefcase. Salome carried only her purse and a small paper bag.

Whittaker did the driving, hanging back a discrete distance, grateful for the winding coastal road. That the church was the couple's destination didn't come as a surprise to the agents—aside from an association with John Whiteside Parsons, religion was the only thing the mathematician and the cleaning lady had in common—though it *was* odd for congregants to visit this early in the morning. According to the SPEAR dossier on the cult, masses were reserved for midnight. Five minutes after the targets entered the church the agents debated getting out of the car to check the ground floor windows, but before they could make a move, the couple reemerged. The only observable change was that Salome no longer carried the paper bag.

"What do you think?" LeBlanc said. "Incense?"

Whittaker answered with a grunt and put the idling car into gear. "Bet you a deuce the next stop is the oracle."

LeBlanc checked his watch. "Before noon? The parlor won't be open."

Whittaker looked away from the rusty black Hudson long enough to give his partner a pitying look. "It's always open for Starry Wisdom. You want to put money on it?"

LeBlanc shook his head. "No. You're right."

"They head south, it's the oracle; north it's her house. I don't see a third option this time of day."

"He could take her out for breakfast."

Whittaker laughed, but LeBlanc was serious. He was always funniest when he was being serious.

"What? Is it out of the question?"

The Hudson stopped at the intersection, then turned left. South. Whittaker pulled away from the curb and followed. "Today's the day, LeBlanc. I can feel it. Time for the chair."

Twenty minutes later, they stood in an empty unit of a three-story brick building on Pine Avenue, Whittaker smoking and pacing while LeBlanc held the bell of a stethoscope to the wall. SPEAR rented the room next to Madam Gamal's Fortune Parlor under the name of a fake accountant. The previous tenant, a dentist, had taken most of his equipment with him when he moved out, but the chair, bolted to the floor, was left behind. The stethoscope didn't come with the room; that was LeBlanc's idea. The fortune-teller's unit was wired for sound, but the microphones only worked when their subjects were talking in what had been the main parlor when the technicians drilled the holes. The old woman changed it up shortly after the installation and now did most of her predicting in a smaller, curtained off space the mics couldn't reach. Whittaker and LeBlanc were still waiting on a tech to drill new holes, but Madam Gamal had taken to living in the shop full time after breaking off her engagement to the painter she'd been shacking up with. Whittaker wondered if she'd changed which room she gave readings in because her sixth sense told her someone was listening in or just because the convertible bed was in the big room.

LeBlanc shot Whittaker a scolding look and waved him away from the notepad he kept on a music stand. The stand provided enough support for him to scribble notes with one hand while holding the bell of the stethoscope to the wall with the other. And he could move it along the wall with minimal noise and effort while following the sound of a subject's voice. Whittaker got the message: he was hovering again, distracting LeBlanc. He stopped trying to read the chicken scratch on the pad and wandered into the empty kitchenette. There was nothing in the fridge but a bottle of cola and some Chinese takeout containers from their last visit. He uncapped the cola. Flat as the Southern California station chief's new secretary. He took a swig anyway and grimaced. LeBlanc appeared in the doorway looking like an intern straight out of med school—stethoscope around his neck, pad in hand, anxiety writ large on his pale face. "She's wrapping it up," he said. "They'll be on the move soon."

"You get anything?"

"Not much."

"Told you today's the day. Let's nab him in the hall and drag him in here."

"What about the girl?"

Whittaker produced a pair of black hoods from his jacket pocket, ever at the ready for such occasions. LeBlanc looked at the fistful of black fabric and his face contorted with...what? Horror? Little late in the game for that.

The thin man spluttered. "What...What about Madam Gamal? You grab two of her clients and drag them into the room next door, that's the end of this. He waved a hand at the empty unit. "We can never use this place again once they know we're next door. Are you nuts?"

"Come on, Jeremy. They already know we're watching them. He has the briefcase on him now and we might not get another shot. The location has served its purpose."

LeBlanc moved to a black phone on a short, round table.

"What are you doing?" Whittaker was already at the door, listening for voices in the hall.

"I'm calling station. We're not blowing cover without authorization."

Whittaker sucked his teeth in disdain, shook his head. "We're not blowing cover. They're gonna be hooded. Get your cuffs ready. You take the girl."

LeBlanc shook his head. "This is not our assignment."

"The assignment is to collect intelligence!" He lowered his voice. "We need to see what's in that case and interrogate them about it. Two prime subjects in one place. You're not gonna get a better opportunity."

"I disagree."

"Put the ameche down and get your cuffs out."

"It's too soon."

"We saw a goddamn monster halfway through the veil last night. We need straight dope before it's too late."

LeBlanc set the handset back in its cradle.

"I'll nab them both if you're not helping, and damn the hoods."

Whitaker opened the door a crack and set his ear to the gap. LeBlanc took the handcuffs from his jacket pocket. They had practiced the move in drills in an L.A. warehouse. The key was not getting hung up on the hood sweep. If you were doing a solo blackout grab, fiddling with the hood could delay seizing the arms and getting the wrists cuffed behind the target's back. Every second that the target had free hands was an unacceptable risk. It was better to have two men per target, but with a girl and a bookworm, Whittaker was more worried about LeBlanc fumbling the move than the likelihood of a counter attack.

The fortune-teller's apartment door creaked open. Pleasantries were exchanged. The door closed and latched. Footsteps on the hall tiles, the clacking of Salome's heels. Whittaker opened the door. No other tenants or patrons in the corridor. About fifteen paces remained until the targets reached the elevator. He gave LeBlanc's shoulder a shove to get him moving and fell in step behind, wanting to time his own attack in relation to his partner's. LeBlanc took one of the hoods and shook it out. One thing you could say for the guy, he moved with a quiet step.

Salome sensed them first, ticking her head to the side as they came up in her peripheral vision while Abdelmalek pressed the elevator button. LeBlanc swept the hood overhead, but the cuffs jingled in his hand, and Abdelmalek ducked out of range at the last second. Whittaker heard the woman cry out—a sharp sound cut short—as he slammed her companion into the steel elevator door, pinning him to it with graceless weight. The Iraqi was small but sinewy, surprisingly strong under pressure, but ultimately no match for Whittaker. The sounds of handcuffs ratcheting and the muffled vocalizations of a woman with not only a hood but also a hand over her mouth reassured him that LeBlanc had his half under control.

Whittaker dropped his own cuffs and hood into his jacket pocket and snaked his thick arms around Abdelmalek's neck, locking him in a sleeper hold that kept him from turning to glimpse his assailant's face, squeezing the man's carotid artery until he blacked out.

Salome kicked at LeBlanc while Whittaker hoisted Abdelmalek's unconscious body over his shoulder and carried him into the abandoned dentist's suite before returning to fetch Salome, who had slumped to the floor like a sack of flour in a passive effort to make moving her more difficult. It wasn't difficult for Whittaker. "Take the briefcase," he told LeBlanc. "And her shoe."

There was a fair chance the fortune-teller had heard something, but her door remained closed. Passing it, Whittaker was sure of only one thing: If Madam Gamal had seen this coming, she hadn't warned her visitors.

* * *

LeBlanc checked Abdelmalek's pulse while Whittaker tied him to the chair. The silk hood stirred where it covered the man's nose and mouth, indicating shallow breathing. Once the prisoners were secure, Whittaker placed the briefcase on a countertop, popped the latches, and riffled through the papers. The woman, also hooded, was tied to a kitchen chair. Whittaker had turned her around to face a wall and pulled her hood up enough to tie a tight gag over her mouth. LeBlanc could see her hands hanging like claws through the gap in the chair behind her back, could see his handcuffs where they squeezed her wrists, blanching her dark skin milky white.

"Jeremy. Look at this."

Whittaker held an ornately carved dagger in his sweaty mitts. LeBlanc's stomach lurched at the sight of the blackwashed silver tentacles showing between the man's hairy fingers. On the counter beside the open briefcase: Documents. Diagrams. Things he could focus his analytical mind on. That was good. It would ground him, maybe ward off the nausea. The struggle in the hall had been brief, but it had left him overheated and struggling to catch his breath. It was the stupid suits. Who wore suits in California in July? Especially when the only people they were likely to interact with would have bags over their heads. The idiocy of government work never ceased to amaze him.

He studied the spread of loose pages laid out on the Formica counter. Most were mimeographed copies of sketches, a bestiary of gods. One jumped out at him—the crustacean warrior they'd seen last night. Lung Crawthok. Some of the pages were originals on moldering paper. These bore images of marine monsters set against swathes of blue-black ink deeper than anything the mimeograph process could reproduce. SPEAR had encountered the material before on other Starry Wisdom documents. The lab in Boston identified it as a previously uncatalogued variety of cephalopod ink.

Whittaker held one of the mimeographed pages. He tapped a knobby finger against a diagram depicting a star made up of daggers surrounded by runes. "Some kinda weapon," he said. "Can you decipher it?"

He looked at the runes and shook his head, then looked at the woman slumped in the kitchen chair. For all appearances, she might have been as unconscious as her companion, though he knew she wasn't. He leaned close to Whittaker and whispered, "We have the case. We could take their money, too, and just leave them here with the door open. The fortune-teller will find them, cut them loose. They might take us for thieves."

Whittaker grimaced. "This is an interrogation, pal. We didn't blow the location just to scamper away. Get hard or get out." Whittaker opened a cabinet and removed another attaché case. Its gleaming aluminum provided a striking contrast to the battered leather briefcase that lay gutted beside it. He scrolled through the combination lock and raised the lid to reveal a device that bore a passing resemblance to a clothes iron connected by a black wire to a battery box. The V43 Mineralight. He flicked a switch on the handle, causing a pool of violet light to spill over the countertop.

"Now we're cooking with gas. Get to it, professor."

LeBlanc fished his flip pad out of his jacket pocket. It was crumpled from the altercation in the hallway. He tossed it on the counter, found a blank sheet, and set about sweeping the light over the ink-stained page fragments. Hidden messages glowed white in the UV light. Boston had also identified the invisible ink used by a secret faction within the Starry Wisdom Church: A combination of blood and semen rendered visible by the wavelength the hand lamp designed for field fluorescence of gems and minerals projected.

The page fragments contained what appeared to be pieces of a prophecy. Whether they pertained to a series of events, or were pieces of a whole, was unclear.

At the hub of the wheel, on the hill soaked with blood
In the year nineteen, in the wake of the flood
The Haunter of the Dark shall arise
And ascend the stair to the ink-stained skies

Another page:

Those who would see must first hear the voice
Who suffer now will later rejoice
First comes the herald, the saint at the bath
Then follows the prophet of music and math

The third page revealed a single line and a set of coordinates.

The priest of the deep shall wake from his sleep: 47° 9′ S, 126° 43′ W

Reading over his shoulder, Whittaker grunted in disdain at the poetry. He opened a drawer and produced another, more primitive tool for extracting hidden information—a pair of pliers. "Come on. Help me get his stompers off."

* * *

At the hub of the wheel
on the hill soaked with blood
In the year nineteen
in the wake of the flood
The Haunter of the Dark shall arise
And ascend the stair to the ink-stained skies

Those who would see must first hear the voice
Who suffer now will later rejoice
First comes the herald, the saint at he bath
Then follows the prophet of music and math

The priest of the deep
shall wake from his sleep
47°9'S, 126°43'W

Abdelmalek jerked awake to find his arms and legs bound. He was in some kind of reclining chair, his head cupped by a firm support. But he was still in darkness. He blinked, his eyelids brushing against fabric, and remembered the hood. It smelled of mold and peppermint. Where had they brought him? How much time had passed since the ambush at the elevator? There was no way of knowing. It seemed unlikely he'd been out for long unless they'd drugged him, and how would he know if they had? A needle prick wouldn't leave a sting. Was he even in the same town? The same state? He didn't feel groggy or cotton-mouthed. Where was Salome? Where was the briefcase?

His shoes off, they removed his socks. How many of them were there? Did it even matter? He was bound to a chair. Even one man could do to him whatever he liked. But it was most likely two; the pair he'd seen lurking around Jack's house. Some kind of law enforcement. The church had been under federal scrutiny for years, ever since the raid on their sister sect in Innsmouth.

"He's awake," a familiar voice said.

"We've been through your papers, Mr. Abdelmalek." A gravely voice. Probably the big man. "Yes, we know who you are. We know you went to the oracle today looking for clarity on some big questions. Well, we have some big questions, too. It's up to you how hard we will have to work to get answers, but we *will* get them."

"Where is Salome?" he asked through the hood.

"She's fine. Don't you worry."

A muffled groan reached his ears. She was here with him, wherever here was.

"I'm not a communist. I came to America for an education, to have a career."

"You sided with communists in the uprising, but it's your religious affiliation that concerns us."

"The Starry Wisdom is a philosophy of peace—"

"Don't give me that. You belong to an apocalyptic cult known as the Order of the Crawling Chaos."

"My religious practices are protected by the first amendment."

"Not if they endanger others, they're not. What are you and Jack Parsons working on? What's your goal?"

The men had let go of his feet while the gravel-voiced one questioned him. Now he felt his right foot seized around the ankle. Cold metal brushed his big toe and a tool gripped the nail.

"We know you're summoning dark gods. We know you've achieved partial manifestations. And we know that your lady friend has made that possible. It's her voice, isn't it? She can chant notes that you and Jack can't. And it's not just because she's female. Isn't that right? Marjorie Cameron engaged in sex magic with you perverts, but with her, you could only raise things in a mirror. Now, if you want to keep your toenails, you will answer my question, because I'm only going to ask it once. One question, one toenail. When I run out of toenails, we move on to teeth. What makes Salome special, and are there others like her?"

It was probably a bluff. Americans didn't torture people. They had underestimated him, thinking he would fold at the first threat of pain. And he would never give them a reason to harm Salome or damage her voice. Her gift was genetic; it couldn't be replicated. She was the closest the church had come to a tangible evocation in generations, thanks to Jack's incense.

A heavy hand struck his face through the hood and he squealed like a whipped dog, more from surprise than pain. A watch ticked in his ear. "You have five seconds to answer."

The five seconds elapsed. The sound of the watch faded. The pliers cracked his nail and he struggled to kick out, but the hand around his ankle was too tight. He tried kicking the pliers away with his other foot, but his calves were bound tightly together.

It was quick when it happened, the nail ripped out in a streak of white fire that tore through his body from toe to scalp as he screamed.

When the flare of pain faded enough to let other perceptions return, he became aware of the warm, slick sensation of blood running between his toes. He writhed in the chair to no avail as the pliers gripped the nail of the next toe.

"No. Wait...you don't have to do this. You misunderstand what we are. We can talk about it...we can talk."

"Then start talking, Abe. But only in answers to my questions. Or we're gonna see if this little piggy goes *wee-wee-wee* all the way home."

He was hyperventilating now, not drawing enough oxygen through the musty silk. Maybe he would pass out. He made a silent prayer to Nyarlathotep that he would. Nearby, he could hear Salome groaning through her gag.

"Don't...please..." It was all he could get out.

"Question two: What is the Fire of Cairo? Is it a weapon?"

He let out a grunt.

"Yes or no is okay for starters. Is it a weapon?"

"Not like you think."

"You don't know what I think." The pliers released and reclamped. This nail was smaller, shorter, harder to get a grip on. "Explain."

"It's not dangerous to people...only to gods."

"And it's a gold scarab?"

He nodded. "Yes."

The muffled sounds from Salome became urgent, an incoherent warning.

"Where is it?"

"I don't know. Lost. It's been lost for ages."

"But you're looking for it. Why is that?" His tormentor's voice changed direction for an aside to his partner. "I think he's withholding." Then, directly again, "Why would you be seeking a god killer?"

"We preserve the old knowledge."

"And if you found the scarab, would you preserve that, too? I don't think so. If it's what you say it is, I think you'd destroy it. But I don't think you've suffered enough to sing true."

The grip tightened. "Question three: What is the purpose of the black mirror?"

"I don't know what you're talking ab—*AAAaagh!*"

"Nine months ago, you removed it from the Starry Wisdom Church in Los Angeles and brought it to Jack Parsons. What is its purpose?"

Abdelmalek focused on his breathing. His racing heart made it difficult to slow the rhythm.

"What is the purpose of the black mirror?"

Breathe in. Breathe out. Breathe in. Praise be to Nyarlathotep.

Pain exploded from his foot in jagged stars. He tasted blood from biting his tongue. The hood was tugged away from his mouth and someone squeezed the hinge of his jaw, forcing it open.

"I lied. We're not waiting until we run out of toe nails."

The tool burrowed between his lips and knocked against his teeth. He tasted blood and rust, bitter metal. Hands held his head as the pliers gripped a molar.

"What role does the Order of the Golden Bough play in your plans?"

Abdelmalek moaned around the tool, shaping the sound into something that resembled a desire to speak. Here, finally, was a question he could answer without betrayal. His tormentor removed the pliers. "No role. We have no connection."

"Bullshit. We know a member of the order arrived at Parsons' house last night. Are you training her to perform similar evocations in New York?" The tool whacked his temple through the hood. "Speak!"

"She's just some student Jack met on the beach..."

"Bullshit. We tracked her from New York. I'm going to ask one more time: What is her role in your operation?"

The pliers penetrated his mouth again, fishing for a tooth. A jangling phone rang, reverberating off the walls in an adjacent empty room. The tool withdrew and the other man—the non-smoker—answered it.

"Yes?"

A pause. He could hear the heavy breathing of his tormenter beside him.

"Yes, sir. We have it. There were hidden inscriptions on the pages."

Another pause for a question followed by an answer muttered softly. The handset clattered into the base. When the man spoke again, he was in the room addressing his partner. "Cut them loose. We're supposed to let them go."

"*What?* We're just getting warmed up here. What did you say? That I'm not getting anywhere?"

"No. They just want the briefcase. No subjects in custody."

"This isn't custody. We're not finished."

"Take it up with the boss. We don't have all the pieces of the puzzle. Let's pack this up."

Abdelmalek heard a drawer slide open. A moment later a shadow fell over the dusky light that reached him in the hood and a needle pricked his neck. A deeper darkness fell quickly.

11

Something called to Catherine from the bookshelf, something magnetic and malign. It tugged gently at her blood in a way that reminded her of the meteorite at the museum. Only that wasn't quite right. This felt more like standing in the cross draft of two open windows on an icy winter day. She focused on the sensation and tested its reach, walking away from the books, toward the workbench where Jack was measuring his powders. The link gradually weakened, then fell away entirely.

Jack showed no interest in which tomes she perused or which objects on the mantle she examined. He had given her free reign to explore the books and artifacts that covered the shelves. Among the hanging swords and knives that adorned the walls were statuettes of Egyptian gods and even a painted wood carving of an Aztec calendar, but all of these were the sorts of reproductions one could find in a tourist shop.

Nor were the books rare. There were interesting titles to be sure, but nothing truly antiquarian. Most had been published in England by Crowley. She hadn't encountered many modern occult treatises before, so these were a curiosity. But despite Jack's wealth, he hadn't acquired any of the rare editions she'd found in the universities and museum libraries of New York. If he possessed a copy of the *Mortiferum Indicium,* he was keeping it well hidden.

She wondered about the chemical experiments he was engaged in. Testing the properties of his ingredients with solutions and tabs of paper that changed color on exposure. Measuring and mixing. Crushing with mortar and pestle. He claimed these were more of his smoke powders—designed for scent and texture and intended to provide a physical medium for the manifestation of spiritual entities. In close proximity to the workbench, she idly wondered if a mistake on his part might cause an explosion. But her subtle senses told her that the real danger in the room was coming from the bookshelf, regardless of the mass-produced titles.

"You feel it, don't you?" Jack said without looking up from his work.

Catherine stared at him until he met her eyes with a faint smile. "Candy always sensed when it was near," he said. He tapped out a measure of some yellow powder onto a sheet of blue paper, then stepped away from the table and reached past her to pull a large, hardback from a shelf of mathematic textbooks. She had glossed over this shelf related to his scientific work, but when he opened the cover she saw the inside of the book was hollowed out, a secret compartment cut through the block of pages. It appeared to be filled with a bundle of white silk, which Jack now removed and unwrapped, revealing a disk of polished black glass. As he stepped toward her with it, a cold wave wafted through her. She recoiled, crossing her arms across her chest and cupping her elbows in her hands.

"Abdelmalek would have a heart attack if he knew I was showing it to you, but it called to you. That means you're meant to look into its depths. It wants to show you something."

"I'm not sure if I want to see. I just…I don't feel well, Jack."

He studied her face, nodding at what he saw. "It's powerful. You need time to get acclimated to it."

"Put it away. Please."

But he made no move to cover the black glass. Catherine resisted the urge to look into the obsidian void, but could not avoid the sensation that it looked into her.

"It's what brought you here. Don't you see? Your dream. This is what you were meant to find. And it makes sense. You're to be my new scarlet woman."

"I don't know what that means."

"The gods Candy catalogued—she saw them in this."

He went to the kitchen table and swept the papers aside, then placed the mirror in a wire bracket, propping it up at a shallow angle. The sketches on the table were horrible enough, but they at least froze the abominations in time, filtered them through the eye and hand of an artist. There was no doubt that Marjorie Cameron was gifted, but it was still art, not so different from the hellish visions of Heironymous Bosch. The prospect of seeing such things directly was another matter altogether. And yet, she found her body drawn to the chair Jack had slid back from the table, found herself sitting and peering into an infinitely deep darkness. Because she *had* to see, had to know if there was more than myth and shared psychosis at work here. She had seen something in the night, in the smoke. But she'd also been sleep deprived— and who knew what drugs might have been burning in the incense powders?

She tore her gaze from the glass and looked at Jack. His eyes were alight with anticipation and a kind of hunger. But the focus of that hunger wasn't the mirror; it was her...and what she might see in it. "Doesn't it require some kind of spell first?"

He shook his head and ran his fingers over his thin mustache. "Only to invoke a specific entity. Right now, I think it wants to show you something." His voice was quiet, as if he didn't want to disturb a process that was already unfolding. And maybe it was. She could feel the magnetic pull pulsing from the glass, tugging at her mind. The air around the disk shimmered, and she felt another sensation, an alien scrutiny.

A silver cloud swirled in the black glass. She let her eyes track its motion and felt herself drifting into a trance not unlike the hypnagogic state before sleep. Subtle imagery emerged from the cloud, textures that resembled coarse fur, pallid flesh, the ridged curve of a goat's horn. She knew Jack hadn't moved from his place at the table, but her sinuses were flooded with an overpowering musk, a dank animal stench that made her gorge rise.

The front door of the castle flew open and Catherine jumped in her seat, her trance broken. Jack was on his feet, moving toward the intruder, raising placating hands as Abdelmalek lurched across the room, wild-eyed and sweaty. He came at her with the intensity of man moving to douse a fire before it can spread, shrugging off Jack's hands, an effort that almost cost him his balance and sent him sprawling on the floor. But he recovered and limped to the table. His chin and the collar of his white shirt were crusted with dried blood. Had he been in a car accident? He reached past her and slammed the mirror facedown on the table, then spun around to seize her by the shoulder, tilting her chair back on its rear legs. Jack snapped out of his confused paralysis at the sight. "Stop it! What's gotten into you? What *happened* to you?"

"Get out!" Abdelmalek shouted at Catherine. From her position in the chair, he towered over her, threatening to spill her backward onto the floor. He jabbed a finger at the open door he'd come through mere seconds ago. "You can go back to the white coven and tell them they will know our secrets when Cthulhu rises!"

Jack grabbed him by his bloody lapels and pinned him against a wall. Catherine's chair touched down again, but she was already on her feet, retreating from the men and the mirror.

"What the hell is wrong with you?" Jack yelled.

Abdelmalek grimaced, his face contorted with disgust, nostrils flaring with rage. It was clear the effort to intimidate her had used up what little strength he had left in the aftermath of an ordeal.

"She's a fucking spy, Jack. A spy! And you're showing her this?" He gestured at the mirror.

Jack released his grip on the man and looked him over—the blood on his shirt and face, at the way he slumped awkwardly against the wall. "Who did this to you?"

"The spooks I told you about. The ones I saw watching the house. They jumped us in the hall at Madam Gamal's. Dragged us into an empty room and tortured me."

Jack looked shocked. "Christ, Kamen. What about Salome? The bayb–"

Abdelmalek cut him off with a look. "She's okay. They didn't hurt her. They dumped us on the street and I took her home."

Jack turned to Catherine with a new hardness in his eyes. She knew she should be edging toward the door but was frozen in place. She *was* afraid, but the more calculating part of her was willing to wager that they would only throw her out—and she wanted to collect every clue they might spill in her presence before that happened. What could they do to her? They were being watched by the authorities.

"You're one of them?" Jack said. "You're with the FBI?"

"They're not FBI, Jack," Abdelmalek said. "And she's not one of them. She belongs to the Golden Bough."

Jack shook his head, as if trying to clear it. "That makes no sense. They're like the Freemasons. Men only."

"The agents that grabbed us, they tracked her in New York. They said the Golden Bough sent her. They think we're working together." He scoffed.

"And you believed them? These men who tortured you. If they're not FBI, who are they? Maybe *they're* Golden Bough. Maybe they're trying to turn us against each other."

"They're some kind of secret police, Jack. I know their kind. No matter the country; those guys are the same everywhere."

But Jack wasn't listening anymore. He was studying Catherine with dark intensity. "You said you saw this house in a dream. Was that true? Are you even a student, or was that a lie, too?"

He moved toward her, his face hard with anger, but she held her ground, raised her hands in a placating gesture.

A scraping sound reached her ears, signaling the animal part of her that she'd miscalculated her chances in the lion's den, and when she flicked her eyes toward Abdelmalek he was brandishing a long knife he'd taken down from the wall. She didn't know the name for it, but it looked Philippine, with a nasty leaf-shaped blade, rusted from the salt air.

"I'll tell you everything if you calm down, Jack. I'm an Anthropology student at Barnard, just like I said. I was approached by someone from the Golden Bough because of my sensitivity, that's true. They know you're doing something real out here. I don't know how they know that, but they asked me to find out what it was. I don't know about your rivalry with them. I don't understand it. You're both looking for the same thing...ancient wisdom...something transcendent. I would think you'd be on the same side."

"That's not what you said when we met on the beach. You said you saw this house in a dream and then just stumbled on it. Like it was providence. You lied to me, Catherine." His eyes roved to the Persian rug in front of the hearth and he winced. "You've been prowling around my house. What else did you see?"

"Jack. Look at me. You want to know what I dreamed? Ever since I was a little girl, I dreamed of finding a true magician. In a castle by the sea. I'd go looking for that no matter who sent me to find it. My whole life, I've suspected there was more to the world than what you could see on the surface. My only loyalty is to my search for the truth."

Abdelmalek had crept close to her. He smelled of stale sweat and the metallic tang of spent adrenaline. The flat of the blade brushed against her leg. "You can't trust her, Jack. There's too much at stake. We're so close now." His voice was husky—the voice of man who has screamed too loud and too long—but the warning in it spoke loudly of secrets she had yet to uncover.

"Jack..." Catherine began. But he wasn't listening to her. His eyes narrowed and she heard the low rasp of a car prowling past the house.

His eyes flicked to the blade. "Get out," he said. "Don't come back."

"Jack..."

"Get out!"

12

Back at the beach cottage, Catherine sat on the bed in a white t-shirt with a towel wrapped around her hips, her hair still wet from the shower, contemplating the phone. She should have called Hildebrand as soon as she reached the cottage, but her emotions were running too high at the time. The long walk across the beach had burned some of the edge off her nerves, but as much as she knew she needed to warn him that the Starry Wisdom was onto them, she also wasn't ready to explain how badly she'd cocked the whole thing up. She'd needed to wash the acrid smell of incense out of her hair first and collect her thoughts: How to frame the situation, what move she might suggest next, and how to convince her mentor that she could still accomplish what she'd come here for.

At least Jack and Abdelmalek were too angry to take a methodical approach to her expulsion from the castle. They hadn't searched her, hadn't found her camera or the spiral note pad that now lay on the bedside table next to the phone. She glanced at the clock and did the math. It would be 4:30 PM in New York. If she didn't call the museum soon, she was liable to miss him. She flipped the pad open to the back cover where she'd inscribed the direct line to his office, then dialed the operator to connect her. After a brief exchange with the receptionist in the museum's administrative offices, Hildebrand came on the line and accepted the charges.

"Catherine. Are you safe?"

"Yes."

"Have you been able to ingratiate yourself to our friend?"

"Yes. Things have happened quickly. I've learned a lot in a short time, but I'm afraid my cover is blown."

"They know I sent you?"

"Not you, specifically. The order. You're being watched. There's some kind of government agency spying on both the Starry Wisdom and the Golden Bough… probably the OTO as well."

"We are aware of that."

Catherine scoffed. "You could have mentioned that. Did you consider that I might not want to get blacklisted before I even graduate?"

"Please accept my apologies for not making the risk explicit, but if one is going to meddle in the affairs of secret societies, my dear…well, one must accept the likelihood that one is being watched. How did Parsons learn you're one of us?"

"Abdelmalek, the mathematician he's working with was interrogated by these government goons. They told him."

"Why would they do that?" The question sounded rhetorical, as if he were musing aloud.

"To isolate Jack and the threat his work poses, I imagine. To make sure the Golden Bough can't pick up where the Starry Wisdom left off if they shut Jack down before he succeeds in opening a portal."

"That may be. And in your estimation, is he close?"

"I've seen things I didn't believe possible. He's making powders that enable partial manifestation of dark gods. But it depends on certain vocal overtones to work. Chants. I don't understand it." She told Hildebrand about the obsidian mirror and the photos she'd taken of the scarab pages from Abdelmalek's cache of Starry Wisdom documents. "I think the pages are from a copy of the *Mortiferum Indicium*, but if they have a bound copy of the whole book at the castle, they're keeping it hidden."

"You've done well, Catherine. Do you think you can do more?"

She looked out the window at the beach where children and a black dog splashed in the surf. "I don't know. This is a lot weirder than I expected. I thought I'd just be flirting with a mad scientist and trying to get a look at his library, but…what do I do if these agents pick me up?"

"Tell them the truth, that you're trying to stop the Starry Wisdom from unleashing an apocalypse, just the same as they are. If they've had any success in surveilling us, they should know that's true."

Catherine considered this. "There's more," she said. "There's a woman who might be important. Has your mole in LA mentioned someone named Salome?"

"I don't believe so."

"I'm not surprised. She's from a different branch of the Starry Wisdom church. Long Beach. The chanting I mentioned, that activates the smoke. She's the key to that. Her voice is unique. I've never heard anything like it. Also, I think she might be pregnant, if that matters."

Was that an intake of breath on the line, or just the sound of the phone handset scuffing against Hildebrand's beard? A few seconds of silence unspooled. At last he spoke. "Can you learn more? Are you willing to try?"

A strong part of her wanted to tell him no, that she was packing for the next flight back to New York, that all of this spy craft was more than what she'd signed up for. But another part of her, the part that had felt not only fear, but a rush of adrenaline and metaphysical awe sitting in Jack's kitchen mere inches away from a window to another world, held that voice down. "I may be able to patch things up, convince Jack my loyalties have shifted."

"I'm pleased to hear it. Don't endanger yourself…"

"Too late."

"But if you can obtain the mirror, do so. Failing that, it would be best to destroy it."

"I think Jack's chemistry set is more dangerous than the mirror. In the glass, they can only appear. They can't pass through."

"Yes, but they can *instruct* him, and that is the source of his progress."

"Okay. I'll see what—"

Knuckles rapped on the weathered cottage door, not loud, but firm and clear. "I have to go. Someone's here."

"Good luck, Catherine. May Kephri light your way."

Catherine stared at the door, reluctant to move as the line went dead in her hand. When the knock came again, she placed the handset in the cradle, stashed her notepad under the pillow and traded the damp towel for a long skirt.

* * *

The man standing on the threshold wasn't what she expected. He was one of the agents—had to be in a suit like that—but his frame was thin, his empty hands delicate, and his features too soft and intelligent for someone who tortured people for information. She opened the door wider and looked beyond. He appeared to be alone, which made her doubt her first impression. Could this be someone Jack had sent? Then again, in California, she couldn't even rule out an evangelist for yet another fringe cult canvassing door to door.

"Ms. Littlefield." It wasn't a question. This man had seen a photo in a dossier, or had perhaps watched her through binoculars. "I'm agent Jeremy LeBlanc. May I come in?"

"Agent? What agency do you work for? Do you have a badge?"

For the space of a breath, she could tell he was calculating the possible trajectories of the conversation. She tried to convey with her eyes that if he told the truth she might respond in kind. "You haven't heard of it," he said.

"Why don't you rectify that then?"

"SPEAR. It's an acronym."

"What does it stand for?"

"Depends on who you ask."

"And I'm asking you."

"Special Physics Exploration And Research. It was formed during the war to investigate new technological threats. You spent last night at the residence of John Whiteside Parsons. We are interested in Mr. Parsons and his houseguest, the Iraqi mathematician Kamenwati Abdelmalek. I understand that your relationship with these men ended as abruptly as it began. Maybe you'd like to know something about the kind of people you've recently become involved with." She wondered if this statement was meant to apply to her associations on both coasts. He looked around at the beach. "May I come in?"

She thought it might be prudent to insist that they talk outside, but then, nothing she had done since meeting Hildebrand in December had been prudent. She knew he was scanning the beach out of a justified concern that someone connected to Jack and Abdelmalek might see them talking. She stepped aside and let him pass. He removed his hat and stood in the area that served as a kitchen, dining room, and den, looking awkward. She felt a reflexive impulse to offer him something to drink, but decided that if he wanted refreshment he could ask for it. She settled on a kitchen chair and gestured at another. "Please." He sat and rubbed his thumb around the brim of the fedora in his lap. It was too hot outside for a suit. She supposed the shade thrown by the brim of his hat was the only relief he'd had from it while trekking across the beach from wherever his unmarked car was parked.

"Let's not beat around the bush, Mr. LeBlanc. Jack kicked me out because you thugs told him I was a member of a rival religious order when you tortured Abdelmalek. How long have you been following me?"

"Since your first contact with the Golden Bough. December. Letting your affiliation slip in Abdelmalek's presence was regrettable. I would have liked to keep that under wraps."

"Why?"

"I thought we should approach you before making a decision about it. My partner jumped the gun."

"Where is he, anyway?"

"He had another engagement."

"Does he know you're speaking with me?"

LeBlanc laughed. "You know, this is not how it usually goes."

"How does it go?"

"Usually I'm the one asking all the questions when I'm talking to someone whose loyalty to their country is in question."

"My interest in the occult is academic, not political."

"Is that right? Was your participation in last night's ritual orgy academic?"

Catherine's face flushed with heat and she knew her pale skin was competing with her red hair for a moment. "I didn't participate."

"But you watched? In your role as an anthropologist?"

"I think you should leave."

He swatted his hat against his hand and sighed. "Sorry. I'm taking the wrong tack here. My partner, he's a religious man. A Christian. For him, everything is black and white, good or evil. He sees people communing with anything that isn't God and his angels and, to him, that has to be devils and demons."

"And you? You're not religious?"

"No, Ma'am."

"So...you don't believe in any of this? You only care if people are communing with communists?"

"I didn't say that. I believe what I see. But I think categories like gods and devils are far too simple for a complex universe."

"You believe what you see. Have you seen one of these entities made visible?"

"Visible? Yes. Maybe not physical, but certainly visible. They inhabit a dimension adjacent to ours. Close enough to catch a glimpse. My fear is that if Jack is allowed to continue combining his science with the occult lore of the Starry Wisdom, they *will* achieve a physical manifestation. One that can sink its teeth and claws into us."

"I guess it doesn't matter what you call them if they're hungry. Gods, demons, predators..."

He nodded. "We spent a lot of money and manpower during the war trying to understand what our enemies wanted, what they were thinking, what they might do next. Now we have people in the Starry Wisdom Church. I shouldn't tell you that, but we do. On both coasts. From what they've gathered, the belief within the church is that these entities ruled the Earth before the rise of man and they will rule it again after his fall. But those who serve them shall be granted eternal life."

"Sounds like gods and devils after all," Catherine said. She went to the fridge and removed a pitcher of iced tea she'd made after settling in the previous day. She poured two glasses and handed one to LeBlanc. It was probably unwise, to trust him, but there was no denying that he was not what she'd expected from the strong arm of the government. "What do *you* think they are? What do you think they want?"

LeBlanc thanked her for the glass and took a drink, then set it on the kitchen table. He adjusted his tie, took a handkerchief from his breast pocket, and patted his forehead. "In December 1946 Parsons employs

Enochian magic to summon an elemental mate. At first, it seems that all he managed to summon is a violent windstorm. But in the weeks following, as he continues the rituals, he and his housemates experience loud knocks and raps, a power outage, and apparitions of floating lights. At the climax of the operation, Marjorie Cameron shows up on his doorstep."

"Were you watching his house at the time?"

LeBlanc shrugged. "The place was Grand Central Station for Bohemians. There was always someone passing through, someone who'd been exiled like you are now. Some jilted lover willing to talk. Anyway, he and Cameron take things to the next level with rituals to create what they call a *moon child*: A spiritual incarnation resulting from sex magic, but not necessarily the physical offspring of the participants. Jack expects this to result in the birth of the goddess he calls Babalon, somewhere in the world, sometime soon. A dark goddess incarnate, destined to usher in the apocalypse and end the Christian era. And you see, that's the terminology my partner gets hung up on. But consider this: Over the next two years, the floodgates are opened for strange aerial phenomena. In forty-six, we get reports of ghostly aircraft over Denmark and a blue orb in the sky over Portugal. In forty-seven, we investigate strange matter that rained from the sky following similar sightings at Maury Island in Washington State. You may have even read in the papers about the airman who crashed his P-51 Mustang chasing what appeared to be a sentient entity in a steep climb that caused him to black out over Madisonville, Kentucky. Within the government, that one was attributed to a classified type of test balloon, but when *I* picture Thomas Mantell rocketing into the stratosphere, I imagine him in pursuit of a thing like a great billowing jellyfish."

"They called it a UFO," Catherine said. "People think they're from Mars, like in the Orson Welles radio drama. What does any of that have to do with the occult?"

"Parsons is a dreamer, but he is also an engineer, a practical man who has learned hard lessons about how difficult it will be to even attain the moon. He knows that if we share the universe with other intelligent life forms, it makes more sense to call them to us, to open a door in space and time, through which they might enter."

"The chants and incense."

"An apple pie left on the windowsill."

"The sounds they made…I've never heard anything like it."

"That's mostly Salome's contribution. She has a genetic gift, but it's incomplete. There hasn't been a human larynx capable of properly sounding those mantras in over a thousand years. Even with the aid of a choir, she can't achieve a full physical manifestation."

"But with Jack's smoke as a medium?"

"They hope the combination will be enough if it's employed when the membrane between worlds is thin."

"The solstice. I saw it marked on a calendar in Jack's kitchen."

"Yes."

"Will it work?"

"I don't know. If it does, we may pass a point of no return. If they bring the right entity through, then it could call the others. A chain reaction. That's why I'm here. My partner might not agree, but we need your help to sabotage the ritual."

"That doesn't make sense. If Salome is so important, and you know when they're going to do it, why don't you just detain her until the time passes? And don't tell me the constitution is an obstacle. I know what you already did to them, and that was just for information."

"That wasn't me."

"You sure do blame a lot on your partner when he's not around. Did he torture *her*, too? I heard you took them together."

LeBlanc shook his head, his eyes fixed on a blank space on the table.

"She's pregnant," Catherine said. That brought his eyes back to her with fresh intensity.

"How do you know? Did Jack tell you?"

"He let it slip in front of me."

"Abdelmalek must have been pissed."

"He's pretty good at hiding it, but yes, I think he was. Why the secrecy about that of all things?"

LeBlanc had drained his glass of iced tea. Now he picked it up by the rim and absently rotated it, turning over his answer in his mind before giving it. "There's a belief within the church…a prophesy, about a child born to a mother with a gift for the voice, conceived by her while invoking the goddess. According to what we've learned from church documents and surveillance of the current oracle, we know that the child is expected to be born with a full voice."

"The ability to produce a physical presence."

"With no smoke and mirrors. Abdelmalek thinks Salome's child will fulfill the prophecy."

"And Jack?"

"He disagrees. It conflicts with his own apocalyptic vision, specifically the work he and Marjorie Cameron did to bring their Babalon into the world. Remember, he only recently discovered the Starry Wisdom. He has a lot to offer them, but he already had a magical worldview. He's adapting quickly because the results they're getting are so spectacular. But he's not willing to swallow the whole doctrine. I think his disillusionment with Crowley made him a little more discriminating."

"What does SPEAR think? Is the child a threat? What do *you* think?"

"Me? I don't know. I try to remain agnostic about the fine points. As for the organization…it's split. Some think preventing the pregnancy is the only thing that matters."

"And you could have done that. Today."

"I wouldn't allow it. Not yet. Not without more certainty. You asked why we don't just detain her on the solstice. My superiors are debating that. I think we should. It would be the safest course of action."

"But…?"

"There's another faction that wants to let things progress just far enough for us to assess the threat."

"That sounds risky." Catherine almost asked him what he knew about the scarab, the Fire of Cairo. But she reminded herself that she was navigating uncharted waters. LeBlanc was disarming, willing to admit where he was ignorant, doubtful or regretful, and they had fallen easily into the rhythm of a speculative conversation between colleagues. She had to be wary of that. Anything a secret agent said was likely designed to elicit a response or manipulate her relationships to the other players involved. Negotiating the tensions between the Golden Bough and the Starry Wisdom was perilous enough. Adding a spy agency to her calculations made it downright disorienting. "What do you think their chances of success are with Jack's help?"

He sighed. "When Parsons and his cohorts first approached Cal Tech about their rocketry project, they were laughed at, considered cranks. A few years later, he's building engines for Navaho missiles to deliver atomic bombs to the Soviets. Only a fool would underestimate him."

"What is it you want me to do?"

"Get back in with him. Keep your eyes open. Who knows—an opportunity to sabotage the ceremony may present itself."

"And you're going to put your faith in that? The chance that a college girl you just met might see a way to prevent a deadly experiment. I'm no hero. And now I've been exiled."

"You'll get back in."

"What makes you so sure?"

"You have more charm than you know."

"I'll need more than charm to get near their ritual."

He reached into his jacket pocket and removed the silver dagger she'd first seen in Abdelmalek's briefcase. "They'll be wanting that back," he said. "I expect it will serve as your key to the castle."

"And if they suspect I have an alliance with you? Abdelmalek has the black eyes of a shark. I don't doubt he's capable of murder."

LeBlanc placed a second silver weapon on the table beside the firs—a small, chrome handgun. "Keep it on you as a last resort. But don't worry. We'll be watching."

13

Days passed. Catherine swam in the ocean and ate in cafes. She studied the silver dagger and tried to translate the hasty notes she'd made from fragments of the scarab and dagger pages, but her efforts brought her no closer to the knowledge of where in the world the amulet was. To fill in the blanks, she would need to develop the film in the Minox camera Hildebrand had given her, but she wanted to wait until she was back in New York before doing that. Undeveloped, the film was safe from the prying eyes of any who searched her. Still, the problem nagged at her. The Golden Bough had sent her to California to learn one thing, and thus far the knowledge had eluded her while she was entangled in a web of other players. It reminded her of the Rumi poem. *It is as if a king has sent you to some country to do a task, and you perform a hundred other services, but not the one he sent you to do.*

She watched the sun set on the Pacific and gave Jack time to cool off, time to turn his attention to the imminent problem he now faced. His powder might be effective in combination with Salome's voice, but only for a brief window of time when the stars were aligned. According to Agent LeBlanc, there was one other advantage the Order of the Crawling Chaos had included in their calculations for the solstice: the Talon of Nyarlathotep. A dagger sharp enough to rend the veil when the membrane between worlds was thin, facilitating the emergence of a Great Old One. If she presented it to Jack on the day of the solstice, he would have little time to reflect on his stroke of fortune. She handled the gun, unloading and reloading it, making her hand and eye familiar with it. She did not see LeBlanc again, and the phone on her bedside table did not ring.

On July 21, she rose at dawn, showered, and dressed in canvas slacks and a black shirt. She tied her hair back and hid the revolver in a knee high stocking. Then she wrapped the dagger in a scarf, tucked it into her shoulder bag with her note pad and pencils, and set out for the concrete castle.

* * *

Salome opened the door, holding a Turkish cigarette in one lazy hand. It was Catherine's first opportunity to see her up close. She wasn't wearing as much makeup as she had on the night of the ritual, but her full lips and long eyelashes still dominated a face that was not as blemish free as it had appeared by firelight from the balcony. Her hair was swept into the same high wave as before and she wore a green silk kimono over a simple black dress. If she was indeed pregnant, she wasn't showing yet. Salome cocked an eyebrow at Catherine, then called over her shoulder. "Jack. Someone to see you." She twirled away from the door without a word of welcome, leaving it hanging open on its hinges, a passive invitation. Catherine had set one foot over the threshold when Jack appeared in an oil-stained apron, a pair of green-tinted safety goggles hoisted up into the wild nest of his curly black hair.

His boyish face darkened at the sight of her and he moved with sudden purpose, a leather-gloved hand reaching for the oak slab to slam it in her face.

"Wait!" Catherine reached into her bag and thrust the silk-wrapped dagger into his extended hand. She watched uncertainty dawn as he registered the weight and shape of the object. Then he scanned the street and ushered her into the house, closing the door behind her before greedily unwrapping it.

"A peace offering," she said.

"Where did you get this?"

"The agent who took it came to interrogate me as well. I convinced him that the Golden Bough sent me here to interfere with your solstice ritual and that I needed the dagger to do it."

"And he just handed it over and let you go."

"What I told him was close to the truth, so he bought it. "

Jack wrapped the scarf around the dagger again and looked her in the eye. "I don't know what to make of you, Catherine. You were sent here to spy on us. You're not denying it?"

"I told you already. After seeing what you can do, I want to see more. I want to be a part of it. Let me in. Let me help. You're doing things they can only dream of in New York."

He glanced at Salome, perched on a leather couch and painting runes on her nails with indigo polish. She seemed so intently focused on the task that there was no doubt in Catherine's mind she was listening to their every word. Jack ran his hand through his hair and nodded to himself, then spun around and took a cigarette from a pack on his worktable. The space was neater than when Catherine had last seen it. She wondered whether he'd cleaned up his materials because his project was finished or stashed them somewhere in anticipation of a raid. For a moment, he paced the Persian rug, drawing deep lungfuls of smoke and burning the cigarette down to a long plug of ash before stamping it out on the mantle. Then, with the quick motions of one who has committed to a course of action and wants to execute it before he can change his mind, he swept the rug aside to reveal the encircled triangle painted on the floor. Catherine's eye was immediately drawn to something she hadn't noticed when she first saw the symbol through smoke and shadow from the balcony: A brass ring attached to what could only be a trap door.

Salome waved her freshly painted nails to dry them and gave Jack an enigmatic look—not a warning. An inside joke?

Jack slid a finger through the ring and pulled the plank door up, setting it down on the rolled up rug. Stairs led down to a basement lit with paltry electric light. He picked up the wrapped dagger from where he'd set it on the floor and started down the stairs. "Wait here," he said as his head sank below the floor.

Muffled voices droned from the basement. Catherine couldn't make out the words, but the tone of the other man told her all she needed to know as it moved from incredulous to combative before hushing again under Jack's mellifluous persuasions.

"Catherine," Jack called. "Come down."

She descended the steep stairs. The air tasted of mold. A dim room came into view. Her sense was that it ran most of the length of the house, maybe farther, but the bulb suspended above the workbench where Abdelmalek sat only reached a close circumference before giving way to the vague suggestion of shelving units and objects draped with linen. The slow, steady echo of water dripping into a puddle reached her ears from somewhere farther off, reinforcing her sense of a larger space.

Abdelmalek leered up at her with a smile—a crooked thing underpinned by pain he was too proud to show. Laid out on the bench in front of him was the body of a rocket in several pieces—a copper tube with steel fins, a canister that might have been an exposed solid fuel engine, and a cone propped upright in the sort of wire rack that might be used to hold test tubes. A jar of what could only be Jack's incense powder sat beside the cone, the handle of a measuring spoon poking out of it. If she didn't know about the mystical aspect of their plans, she would have thought he was packing an explosive shell with black powder.

Beside the disassembled rocket lay the dagger. Abdelmalek laid a hand on the antique silver hilt. "You made the right choice," he said. "The only choice with a future, anyway. How far did you get in the Golden Bough?"

"Neophyte."

"You believe her, Jack? They sent a Neophyte to infiltrate us?" He laughed, poured another scoop of powder into the rocket cone, then used the blade of the dagger to level it off.

"It makes sense," Jack said. "If she was found out, she couldn't give up the passwords and gestures of the upper grades."

"We have infiltrated their ranks as well," Abdelmalek said. "Who was your sponsor, Hildebrand?"

Catherine nodded.

Abdelmalek sneered. "Such a self-righteous crusader for the light. What a hypocrite."

"How?"

He waved his hand as if shooing a fly. "They believe in the nobility of mankind. They believe that *man* is evolving to godhood, or haven't they told you that yet? They claim to be the progenitors of an ancient lineage of priest-kings who guard a secret seed of enlightenment, a seed of the fruit of the Tree of Knowledge, which will one day be unlocked by the power of science to usher in an age of peace. But it's the same old Christian lie: Man is the favored son of a benevolent creator and deserves dominion over all life on earth. They worship the light!" He laughed. "Did you see what happened four years ago when man unleashed the power of the sun on Japan to end the war? Left to his own devices, man will *destroy* all life on earth." His words slurred slightly and she wondered if he had been drinking or using painkillers to deal with what the agents had done to him.

Catherine didn't know if his was an accurate portrayal of the order's inner doctrine. She'd read enough to know that the esoteric teachings of the Golden Bough were something along these lines, but did the Starry Wisdom really have members who had infiltrated the second gate?

Jack spoke up. "You would renounce the Golden Bough and embrace the Starry Wisdom, Catherine?"

She moved further into the light so he could see her eyes when she answered. "Meeting you was a revelation," she said. "You've made contact with superior intelligences, the aim of every religion in history, and you've done it in a way that's evident to the senses. I've *seen* it. I want to see more."

"It should be the most natural thing in the world to commune with them," Jack said. "But the Black Brotherhood repressed man's primal energies and closed our senses off from the universe."

"Black Brotherhood?"

"The Church and their predecessors. Those who would trade spiritual vision and voice for mundane power over other men. Men who would tolerate slavery for false security rather than aspire to meet the gods eye to eye." It sounded like a well-rehearsed rant. Jack had probably shared it on many a night of drinking with his band of mystics and science fiction writers. SPEAR probably had a transcript of it somewhere.

"What do they want?" she asked. "The gods. Have they told you?"

Abdelmalek scoffed. "What does the sea want? What does a volcano want?"

"To transcend their boundaries," Jack said.

Abdelmalek stroked the engraved dagger again, tracing the line of a silver tentacle. "When they walked the primordial earth, they shared a symbiotic relationship with our ancestors. But for centuries they've been shut out by our fear of the dark, our aversion to the crawling chaos that is life itself and the limits we've imposed on our own eyes and tongues."

"Today that changes," Jack said. "Today we open the way and welcome them home." He put a hand on Catherine's shoulder. "Thanks to you, it's within our grasp."

"How?" She nodded at the dagger. "I brought you that as a show of good faith, but the agent said it was made for *banishing*."

Jack pulled a sheet aside to reveal a shelf stocked with leather-bound books. The titles ranged from English to Latin, Hebrew, Greek, and Arabic. Some spines were blank. Others bore only symbols. Jack selected one of these, a burgundy volume with a parabolic pentagram stamped in gold between raised bands. It fell open to an oft-consulted page in his hands and he set it down on the workbench, away from the rocket parts and powders.

The left page was dominated by a diagram of the dagger, surrounded by the same family of runes she'd seen on the scarab pages in Abdelmalek's briefcase. The right page displayed a catalog of geometric forms with arrows indicating the order in which they should be traced.

"It's a sacred relic of our order," Jack said.

"The Talon of Nyarlathotep," Abdelmalek chimed in reverently.

"A double-edged sword," Jack said, "if you'll pardon the pun. This book describes operations for invoking. There is another, penned by a heretic, that details banishings. The blade may not look especially sharp for cutting flesh, but on another level, an energetic level, it has a keener edge than any other, because it can cut *air*, the very membrane that separates our world from theirs."

Catherine felt a chill course through her body at these words, and Jack nodded gravely at her naked awe. "If that veil is cut at the proper angles, and vibrated with the proper sounds, the gods can be ushered in or cast out."

"Why do you need a rocket, then? If you have this weapon."

"Without the true voice, we need every other advantage we can bring. A Sacred place where a breach has already occurred. A singer capable of producing even partial harmonics. My powder unfurled in the atmosphere to grant substance to the visitor. We had hoped those would be enough, but now, with *this*...if the god appears, we can slice the membrane and bring it through."

"It?"

"Azothoth, the mad piper in the eye of the storm. He will open the way for the others."

"You said the location is sacred. Here, near the ocean?"

"No. A secret place. The place where I had my first encounter with the gods."

"What about the agents? Won't they follow us?"

"If they follow, we'll lose them in the desert with a smoke screen. And if we succeed, we may even become invisible for a time."

Abdelmalek's cheeks glistened in the light of the bare bulb. Catherine realized he was crying tears of joy. "We will see *their* world for a shining moment when I cut the membrane. We will taste the air of the dreamlands. And if those fuckers try to follow us, they will die with it in their lungs."

Catherine swallowed, acutely aware of the cold weight of the pistol against her calf. "When do we leave?"

Jack checked his watch. "Soon. The others will meet us in the Arroyo at dusk. There's just enough time to pack up the equipment and prepare you."

In her mind, she recited a silent prayer that there would be no special clothing required, no bare legs, and for a sickening flash, she pictured the ritualists stripping naked among the rattlesnakes and scorpions and discovering she was armed. "Prepare me how?"

Jack paged through the tome on the workbench and tapped his finger on a couplet rendered in phonetic English. "Can you carry a tune?"

14

Abdelmalek's sedan bounced and rocked over the dirt road, kicking up clouds of dust and startling a jackrabbit across the cracked hardpan to seek cover in the sagebrush. They rode into the Mojave trailed by a small pickup truck that carried the rocket swaddled in blankets, the sun at their backs shining on the distant Providence mountains with the preternatural clarity of long golden rays through thin desert air.

Parked among the Joshua trees, they unloaded the equipment. There were seven in all, a number Jack claimed was auspicious. "The number of letters in the holy name *Babalon*." Before Catherine could ask for elaboration, he was marching off into the desert with the rocket cradled in his arms. Abdelmalek tucked the silver dagger through his belt and followed. Catherine and Salome came next, trailed by two young men and an older woman. Jack had skipped over introductions in his haste to reach the site before full dark. The woman carried a bottle of deep blue glass with a cork stopper, and one of the men bore an ebony staff.

They walked beneath the deepening dome of the sky, not a word uttered between them. Catherine strained against the silence, hoping to hear the distant drone of a motor, certain that LeBlanc and his partner must have tailed them from a careful distance.

Eventually, Jack set the rocket on the ground at a spot with no distinguishing features except for the intersection of two overhead power lines running along what looked like an infinity of poles to the horizon. Beneath the wires, the sound of their humming reminded Catherine of the drone of an aboriginal spirit catcher she'd once seen demonstrated by a musicologist at a museum. It seemed odd that Jack would choose a site with an obstructed sky to launch his rocket, but perhaps the power lines figured into his esoteric calculations. So much of what he believed sounded stark raving mad when he tried to articulate it. If she hadn't seen Salome assume the writhing form of a goddess in that midnight rite, she might have dismissed the whole enterprise as the delusion of a cracked genius. But the fear of what she expected to witness was tangible—and if she was being honest with herself, laced with exhilaration.

Gazing up at the first stars to emerge, she realized with a pang of dread that no one knew where she was. Only two men outside of the Starry Wisdom cult had even the faintest idea of her whereabouts, and of those, one claimed to be a magician and the other a secret agent.

What if she had gambled her life on a miscalculation? Might there not be a sinister reason for the ease with which the Starry Wisdom had welcomed her into the fold? If the dagger was for rending more than a metaphysical veil...if she ended this misguided journey as a sacrificial offering, would her parents be denied even the closure of a corpse? She searched the horizon for a car or helicopter, but found only the circling shadows of raptors.

The man with the staff traced a circle in the dirt about a dozen feet in diameter, while the woman with the blue bottle uncorked it and moved among the group, offering each celebrant a sip. Her manner was ceremonial, the bottle held on the palm of one hand in between tipping it toward the recipient's lips with a phrase whispered in a language Catherine couldn't discern.

"What is it?" Catherine asked Salome, who had just opened her eyes after swallowing. "A tincture of mescal, wormwood, and traditional herbs. It will tune your mind to the right frequency so you can see him when he comes."

Catherine nodded and folded her hands in the same gesture she had seen the others make. The liquid tasted bitter and florid. She closed her eyes and swallowed, hoping she was projecting the proper appearance of gratitude and grace. Jack arranged the rocket on a triangular launch pad emblazoned with white sigils that made it impossible to distinguish how much of the hardware was technical vs. ceremonial. A pair of wires ran from the launch pad to a control box.

The cultists swayed in the circle, their eyes on the deepening sky. Just as Catherine was beginning to wonder when the ritual would begin, she realized it already had. It was a subtle confluence of elements coming together, arising out of motions and sounds that at first seemed unrelated. Her first impression was that the buzzing in the power lines had somehow split in two and dropped an octave to vibrate through the desert floor. She looked at the rocket, expecting it to be the source of the vibration, but it remained inert, the control box untouched, like the head of a dead snake lying in the dust at Jack's feet. Her companions were swaying in rhythm now, Abdelmalek swinging the dagger in long, loping arcs as he moved widdershins around the perimeter of the circle. He looked drunk until she noticed that he never allowed so much as the toe of a shoe to cross the line graven in the dirt.

The others moved inward, allowing Abdelmalek to pass behind them, and Catherine followed suit. As they fell into formation around the rocket, she saw the lips of the man opposite her moving. He was chanting, a low guttural drone. All of the men were. But even this could not account for the low vibration she felt in her feet and bowels. The orange line smudged across the indigo horizon trembled with that same vibration. The scattered stars jittered in the heavens with its thrumming. She became aware that the vibration arose within her own cells even though she had not yet joined in the chant.

Jack knelt and picked up the control box. He grinned at Catherine and rolled his hand in her direction, like the conductor of a choir. A bead of sweat ran from his hairline down the side of his face. Even in the dusk, his eyes shone with a manic light. He was in his element, the two threads of his life's great work finally conjoined, like the power lines thrumming above the circle, and she knew in that moment she was looking at a man with the will and knowledge to blast a hole through the sky. To heaven, hell, or whatever Byzantine abominations lay on the other side. She could hardly bear the intensity of that look. She closed her eyes and took up the chant. The sacrament they'd given her coursed through her nerves. An inner light bloomed behind her eyelids. In a flash, she was back in New York, the dry heat of the Mojave replaced with falling snow. Peter Philips smiling shyly at her, a book under his arm, looking away as he absorbed her assertion that knowledge was power.

"Same tree, different fruit."

Something on the ground hissed like a cobra.

Still singing, Catherine opened her eyes and watched the rocket fly.

* * *

"There!" LeBlanc leaned into the windshield and pointed at the sky. Like he was the only one who could see the phosphor-bright star blazing up from the desert into the heavens. Like he thought Whittaker was blind. Whittaker took his foot off the gas and let the car roll to a halt, his eyes tracing the arc of pale gray smoke back to the ground before it vanished on the rising evening wind. It looked like the launch point was somewhere between the power lines north of the road, maybe five miles from their current location.

The rocket soared out of view beyond the car roof. Whittaker put the gearshift in park and stepped out, watching it climb and, half expecting it to culminate with an explosion of fireworks, though he knew it wasn't that kind of rocket. It was a kind the world had never known, if LeBlanc and the other bookworms were to be believed. Never mind chemical weapons. If Parsons succeeded with this, there would be a weapon that could unleash monsters on the battlefield. The only problem was that Earth itself would be the battlefield and the forces unleashed would be beyond the command of any man. On the other side of the car, LeBlanc tracked the rocket through the viewfinder of his 8mm movie camera. The frames clicked like a noisy stopwatch as he turned the crank. The white flare of the exhaust plume faded into the night followed by a pop like a champagne cork, and a red cloud of smoke. It rained down over the desert in shifting curtains that reminded Whittaker of the northern lights.

"You check your weapon?"

"Of course," LeBlanc said with the closest thing he could muster to annoyance.

"So you have my back. You're sure we don't need to call for a team."

"No. The camera's more important than the gun here. We need to document their experiment."

"So I'm told. Get in the car, Capra."

The red cloud hung lazily in the air as they drove toward it, shifting and wavering in defiance of gravity. Sometimes a violet light seemed to pulse at its heart. From other angles, as the car progressed through curves and slopes toward the valley floor, it seemed to flicker in and out of existence, assuming myriad shapes. Eventually, the tendrils of vapor coalesced into a descending sphere before vanishing entirely when they hit the final stretch of road and rolled up to the place where the rusted sedan and pickup truck were parked.

The air smelled of sulfur, but there was no sign of the cultists except for their abandoned vehicles and a nine-foot circle traced in the dirt of a clearing. Whittaker drew his weapon and approached it.

"Wait," LeBlanc said. "Don't cross the line."

"Why not?"

Leblanc panned the camera across the landscape, then tracked back and focused on the circle for a moment before letting go of the crank handle. Absent the ticking of the film, the only sounds were the susurrus of wind in the Joshua trees and the low hum of the power lines. "You hear that?"

Whittaker frowned. "The power lines?"

"Listen closer. There's a sound inside the hum, like voices chanting."

It was true, there were syllables hidden in the crackling. He couldn't make out the words, but they were there, like the echo of a choir reaching his ears through heavy curtains. He kicked a rock into the circle, expecting...he didn't know what. For it to lose its grip on gravity and float when it crossed the line? But it only tumbled to a stop where it ran out of momentum. "Why did you say don't cross the line?"

"They're inside. In a bubble. Half in this world, half in the other. Pick something in the circle, a focal point to keep your eyes on, and walk the perimeter."

Whittaker focused on the rock he'd kicked. Nothing changed until he'd moved 180 degrees with his eyes trained on it, and then his vision flickered, revealing the ghost of a shoe beside the rock. It disappeared with the next step he took, and he craned his head back until it reappeared and grew: a shoe, a pant leg, the ghost of a man.

Parsons—rapturous eyes aimed skyward, lips moving in sync with the echoes, shaping the long vowel of the power drone into a dirge, a psalm, a song that vibrated the air of an adjacent world. He held a woman's hand, but when Whittaker leaned in to see the rest of her, the scene winked out again. He tried to regain his previous vantage, but no matter how he turned his head now, he saw only empty ground, dirt and rocks. LeBlanc stalked around the other side of the circle, playing the same game of optics. He still held the camera, but the fact that he wasn't rolling footage was proof enough that he hadn't found a view into the bubble.

"Can *they* see *us?*" Whittaker whispered. LeBlanc raised a silencing finger and shot him a look. *I don't know, but maybe they can hear us.*

"This is bullshit," Whittaker said aloud. "I'm going in."

* * *

The sky was a fractal quake of ultraviolet violence sleeting photons from a howling maw at the apex of the dome. Catherine's bones thrummed like tuning forks under the assault. Tears streamed from her eyes into the flame of her hair trailing out behind her. She had ceased singing, but the subtraction of her voice from the cresting song did nothing to diminish it. Salome's melody surged with icy harmonics, cast out across the alien landscape and reflected back from cyclopean towers. Constellations of stars hung above those structures in configurations she had never seen before. Descending from that sundered sky into the sacred circle, a creature of condensed crimson smoke unfurled to reveal a maw of gnashing shards of light flanked by billowing tentacles. She tried to scream, but the sound was sucked away into the maelstrom.

Jack squeezed her hand. Abdelmalek raised the dagger and traced sluggish glyphs in the congealing air. The others swayed to a rhythm she couldn't hear, their mouths forming syllables too swift to decipher.

An intruder crashed into the circle, a bear of a man in a black suit and white shirt, his hat snatched away and necktie tugged aloft as he tumbled into their midst. With his arrival, the energy shifted frequency. The atmosphere snapped taut, and Catherine sensed a malevolent sentience turning its predatory gaze on the man. The ethereal tentacles hardened into sinewy flesh and seized the man, lifting him toward the howling mouth. He squirmed, flailed, and kicked a shoe off. Catherine didn't see the gun in his hand until it went off with a flash, the shot punching through the cacophony. The wrist of his gun arm was squeezed tight in the grip of the beast, causing the shot to go astray.

The sound snapped Catherine out of her trance and she remembered the revolver tucked in her stocking under her slacks. Her hand moved toward it, though her eyes remained fixed on the descending god. It had begun as a nebulous cloud above the desert, but had quickly gained substance as it approached the chanting cultists, fed by the sounds of their song. The stench of it churned her stomach—sulfur, sewage, and ozone. In places, she could still see through its billowing body to the stars beyond.

She forced her eyes from it and scanned the circle. The shot had disturbed the chant, but the old woman picked up again. The flailing man suspended above their heads had managed to twist his body around and free his wrist so that his weapon hand was restrained by a single tentacle fastened around his elbow. He struggled to aim the gun at Salome. The star of this infernal choir, she stood stock still across the circle from Catherine, her features placid, her eyes closed, her voice pouring into the creature's mouth like a transfusion of blood or molten lava. A red tentacle unfurled and coiled around the gun, heating the metal to an orange glow until the agent dropped it to the desert floor where a layer of skin from his hand burned off the handle in a thin scrim of smoke.

Jack's nails bit into Catherine's wrist and she thought the glass of her watch would crack under the pressure. "Sing!" he screamed into her face, then repeated the command to the others "Sing, goddammit!"

The song swelled again, granting mass to the monster. Catherine moved her lips in the shape of the chant and closed her eyes. She couldn't watch. The man was a fly caught in a web and the spider was about to feed. Where was LeBlanc? This poor soul had to be his partner. She knew he wasn't innocent. He had tortured Abdelmalek. She could only guess what else such a man might have done. But did he deserve this?

Abdelmalek appeared beneath the body. He pressed the point of the silver dagger into the base of the man's throat, drawing a bead of blood that ran upward across the man's waxen cheek before it fell away skyward into the gnashing vortex, sending a ripple through the air on contact.

Azothoth came into grotesque focus as if reality itself had been adjusted like a lens. Abdelmalek spun away to the edge of the circle with the grace of a dancer. He raised the dagger above his head, holding it with both hands, and stabbed it through the wavering membrane of light. As he dragged the blade down, the Mojave was revealed through the gash, as if he were slicing through the screen in a movie theater to reveal a backstage world; the place they had come from and to which they would return. And if Abdelmalek had his way, a world that would never be the same again under the power of a new pantheon.

Catherine dropped to one knee and drew the revolver from her stocking. She had never fired a weapon before, never considered killing anyone. How had this fallen to her? Jack looked down at her, his hand still clutching her wrist as she came up with the gun in her hand. His eyes flared at the sight. He pulled her in close, grappling for the weapon, but she flung her right arm out and aimed across the circle at Salome. The man in the air was screaming.

"No!" Jack yelled.

Salome opened her eyes.

Catherine pulled the trigger twice. Salome jerked backward, blood erupting from a ragged hole in her black dress. She staggered a few steps toward Catherine and crumpled to the dusty ground. The atmosphere snapped like a guitar string and the agent came crashing down on his back in the center of the circle. The dome, the creature, and the alien panorama winked out of existence with the severing of the song. The silent desert stretched to the horizon around them beneath familiar stars, marred only by the headlights of a car spilling over the ground and a tall, thin man silhouetted against the glare.

LeBlanc. Catherine scrambled toward him, straining against Jack's grip. She had dropped the gun after firing it. One of the men bent to pick it up, but the agent who had crashed to the earth was already on his feet. He kicked the gun and sent it skittering out of the circle and into the brush, then brought his foot up and kicked the cultist under the chin before turning and throwing a haymaker at Jack that sent him sprawling to the ground. Free of his grip at last, Catherine ran for the light.

LeBlanc shoved her into the back of the car, then braced his forearms on the doorframe and squeezed off a shot at a cultist who had retrieved the revolver from the brush and was aiming it at the car. The engine was already running. A moment later, he was in the driver's seat, fumbling with the gearshift. Catherine sat up and stared out at the scene framed like a diorama in the windshield. Jack held the other agent's gun—now cooled—and fired at the tires, kicking up plumes of dust. Abdelmalek shifted side to side in a low, expectant stance, waving the blade in a restless arc beneath a feral grimace, his dark hair a sweaty curtain over his eyes. Beyond him, the old woman knelt over Salome's body. Catherine went cold at the sight, as if it were her own blood draining out into the cracked earth. She rubbed her wrist and found her watch missing, the chain broken in the struggle.

Then the scene through the windshield was eclipsed by the other agent's bulk. He landed in the passenger seat, rocking the car on its shocks and bumping Catherine's head against the ceiling. Bullets punched through the fenders and pinged off the engine block. Before the big man could pull the door shut behind him, it lurched away as LeBlanc floored the gas pedal, cranked the wheel, and spun the car around in a wide, squealing arc that threw grit at the cultists before leaving them in the dark.

15

Catherine stood at the terminal window and watched the tanker truck pull up to the Boeing Stratoliner, her Western Airlines ticket trembling in her hand. LeBlanc touched her wrist gently and she flinched, reminded of how Jack had gripped it in a claw that she thought would never let go.

"I know it looks impossibly big, but trust me, it's the newest, safest plane you can fly."

She shook her head. "It's not flying jitters." Though she did find the notion that the behemoth sitting on the tarmac could get up into the sky and stay there all the way to New York International a little absurd, she had certainly seen more flagrant violations of natural law in the past twenty-four hours. And no threat of bodily harm bothered her in the aftermath of what she'd done in the desert. She wasn't a religious person, but that didn't prevent her from feeling a self-inflicted spiritual wound as she grappled with the knowledge she had taken the life of a pregnant woman.

"What is it, then?"

She looked at him, incredulous, until he looked away at the hazy Los Angeles skyline. "You did what you had to," he said. "And I have no doubt you saved lives. You'll never know how many mothers and children are alive in that city today because of what you prevented."

"We don't know that."

"I do."

"Your partner, Whittaker...does *he*?"

LeBlanc checked his wristwatch.

"He was horrified that you gave me a gun."

"He came around by the time we filed our report. You don't have to worry about him."

"Do I have to worry that the FBI will come knocking on my door?"

"No. It's taken care of. You'll read about it in tomorrow's paper."

"Oh God."

"Relax. An unnamed college girl was abducted by a cult. She was meant to be used as a human sacrifice in Petroglyph Park near China Lake, but authorities intervened. They'd been conducting surveillance on the cult for un-American activities. They swooped in and saved the girl. One cultist was killed in the raid."

"That's it?"

"That's it. It won't follow you home."

She knew what he meant. But in her heart there would be no outrunning what she'd done. "There was no time to think," she said. "I just acted. And we don't even know if it was worth it, if I prevented anything. They might have failed anyway. You said Salome didn't even have the full voice."

He took her hand and gave it a gentle squeeze. "Whittaker is alive because of you. And I know this isn't easy to hear, but the older woman? She's the oracle Abdelmalek took Salome to see about the baby. We know what she told them. If Salome gave birth, the child would have been born with a larynx capable of bringing every incantation to life."

Catherine recoiled. "You're telling me the government is willing to accept killing a baby to prevent a *prophecy*?" Her voice rose in anger and disgust. He shushed her, put a hand on her shoulder, and led her toward the door to the tarmac, where a stair was being wheeled into place beside the plane.

"Outrage is a luxury for the ignorant, Catherine. I've seen things that give me no reservations or regrets. So have you. You prevented an apocalypse. I don't know if it would have come yesterday or decades from now. But you prevented it. Tell that to your mentor in the Golden Bough."

Over the intercom, the desk attendant announced boarding for New York. LeBlanc picked up Catherine's suitcase and led the way.

"There's one more thing I need to ask you," he said.

"Yes?"

"You came out here to spy on the Starry Wisdom for the Golden Bough. Was there a specific question they wanted you to answer?"

"Like you, they wanted to know if Jack was close to a breakthrough." She paused, unsure of how much detail she wanted to share with a government agent who had spied on both sides of the occult war she'd been drawn into. But then, maybe he could tell her if she'd been pursuing a dead end all along. "I was also tasked with finding out if the Starry Wisdom has possession of an amulet that might serve as a weapon against the Great Old Ones, should they return."

"The Fire of Cairo." LeBlanc shook the suitcase with a grin. "Did you find it?"

"I'm afraid not. I don't suppose you'd tell me if you knew its location?"

"I hate to disappoint a pretty lady before parting, but if it still exists, it's probably not in America."

"Considering how close they came, that's unfortunate."

They had reached the line of passengers forming at the boarding stairs. Looking up at the plane, Catherine rued the prospect of the eighteen-hour transcontinental flight. LeBlanc studied her, still holding the suitcase. "Jack brought you into his confidence for a time. Did you learn anything from him about the scarab?"

Catherine thought of the Minox pocket camera tucked into a rolled up pair of stockings in the powder blue suitcase in his hand. She thought of the photos she'd taken by candlelight of Abdelmalek's grimoire pages. She hoped they would be legible. "I'm afraid not."

If he knew it was a lie, his face didn't betray it. He placed the suitcase on the tarmac at her feet.

"What will happen to Jack now?" she asked. "Will he be in the papers and lose his job again?"

"No. It's a delicate game we're playing and you've only seen the opening round. For now, the decree from on high is that, despite the danger he poses, his work should be allowed to continue."

This came as a shock and she made no effort to hide it. "But...you said we prevented...how can they...they want to *use* him, don't they? Like the Manhattan Project. They want to weaponize his work." The idea sent fingers of frost through her nerves. When the sensation passed, she felt a new and profound gratitude for the maneuvers LeBlanc had performed to secure her a seat on a flight to New York rather than a cell in a secret facility where those who knew too much were kept with their secrets. Though she didn't doubt SPEAR would be keeping tabs on her for the rest of a career she'd hardly begun.

"Thank you, Jeremy." She pecked him on the cheek and watched him blush. "Thank you for seeing me home. Be careful. You seem caught between dangerous people on both sides."

He nodded and touched the brim of his hat. "You do the same, Catherine. Safe travels."

16

On a hot day in August, Catherine Littlefield sat before the Willamette meteorite in the entry hall of the Hayden Planetarium, imagining that every person who passed her was a star, each moving in its own orbit, and all revolving around her. Catherine was a woman with a secret. She had been for some time, but today she finally knew what it was. She had developed the photos and spent the morning deciphering the pages they documented. Both the photos and the notes were in a manila envelope tied with red string in the handbag that rested on the bench at her side. And now here he was—Hildebrand, in a tweed jacket and starched shirt, settling down on the other side of the bag and joining her in meditation on the iron rock.

She could feel its humming in her bones. It reminded her of power lines in the desert.

"I got your note," Hildebrand said. "You had me worried. When did you get back?"

"Three days ago." She touched the envelope jutting out of her bag. "I wanted to be sure of what I had before I brought it to you."

He nodded, but did not reach for the envelope. She wondered if he knew about SPEAR, if he was aware they might be watching. "Would you join me for a walk in the park?" she asked.

"It would be my pleasure."

The last time Catherine had walked these paths with Hildebrand, there had been snow on the ground and not a soul in sight. Now the park bustled with children, couples, and dogs. Her companion didn't ask where they were going, though he had probably guessed after the first couple of turns. At length, the weathered stone of Cleopatra's Needle rose from the green canopy of trees at the crest of the hill.

The monument had attracted only a handful of visitors to its benches. If Whittaker and LeBlanc were characteristic of the breed, none of them appeared to be SPEAR agents. Nonetheless, she linked arms with Hildebrand and spoke in a low voice as they circled the obelisk.

"I didn't find the book. If they have a complete copy of the *Mortiferum Indicium,* they're keeping it hidden. It's possible that the church doesn't trust Abdelmalek with it because of how much he's shared with Jack. The pages I photographed were already copies, probably made on a machine at Caltech. I doubt they have the full text."

"That's unfortunate."

"The pages I was able to photograph contained additions to the original grimoire. The use of a cipher with direct English equivalents is a sure sign of that."

"You've translated this cypher?"

She nodded. "I've been poring over the fragments for days."

"And what have you learned?"

She took a deep breath. "I believe the copy of the *Deadly Amulet* in the possession of the Starry Wisdom was once the property of Henry Hurlbolt Gorringe. His notes about the Fire of Cairo—how to use it, where he hid it—were encoded in his copy of the book. He also made notes about another relic. A dagger that they already possess. I've seen it."

The color with which the walk had infused the man's face blanched away at her words. "The Talon of Nyarlathotep."

"Yes. The photos and my translations are in an envelope I'll leave with you. Deciphering the pages was easy, but I wanted to confirm what I found."

"Does the cipher reference the obelisk? The time capsule under the cornerstone?"

"Not exactly. One of the scarab pages says: *Kephra flees Karkinos at the Rising.*"

Hildebrand surveyed the scant crowd around them, then focused on the base of the obelisk. "Karkinos, Cancer, the crab."

Catherine walked around the monument to the northeast corner.

Hildebrand followed. "I don't understand. The records show that Gorringe buried a secret item in a lead box beneath the cornerstone, where it would be safe baring a cataclysmic event. What do the crabs have to do with it?"

"I think he wanted people to believe the scarab was irretrievable. That's why he didn't just place a box in the time capsule, he also made sure it made the newspapers that he had. He knew that speculation about the contents would preserve the fact. And anyone who knew enough to trace the scarab to him would assume it was there, where no one could verify it, but where anyone would give up the search. He even had the foresight to use a lead box that couldn't be penetrated by technologies like x-rays. Only in his private copy of the *Mortiferum Indicium,* the book containing the history of the amulet and instructions for its use, did he note the actual location, in cypher."

Understanding dawned in Hildebrand's eyes. "Not so far from the red herring." He backtracked around the obelisk far enough to look at the crab in the southeast corner, then returned to Catherine at the northeast. "The mouth cavity of this one is hollowed out. On the other, it's just a carved outline."

Catherine smiled. "The crab that faces the rising sun," she said. Her heart pounded in her chest as she climbed over the iron railing and stepped up onto the limestone base. She slid her fingers between the iron claws, into the crab's mouth, and touched metal. A lose object on a chain. But as she withdrew it, she realized the shape was too familiar. It was a silver lady's watch in an art deco style with a hairline crack in the glass face. She turned it over in her hand, as if any further proof were needed that it was hers, and found the engraving her parents had commissioned.

For Catherine,
Your time has come.

17

In another part of the city, a woman in a burka might have drawn attention, but not in Red Hook, where the streets bustled with immigrants. No heads turned as she made her way among the crumbling red brick tenements accompanied by a short, dark-haired man in a vest and shirtsleeves. Together, they moved silently beneath laundry lines, telephone wires, and burned out street lamps. If anyone noted their presence, it was the women smoking cigars on the fire escapes, and only then when the pair ascended the steps of the old stone church.

The building, which had once served a congregation of the Dutch Reformed faith, had been converted into a dance-hall in the 1920s and had been a venue for basement lectures on eastern philosophy by a Professor Suydam for a time, before the police raided it following a string of child abductions amid rumors of black magic. Apparently the authorities broke up an illegal immigration and human trafficking ring that depended on subterranean waterways and a network of catacombs beneath the church. For a time, the building sat deserted and boarded up. The alleged tunnels were said to have been filled, but no one could attest to witnessing the trucks and work crews such an endeavor would have called for. Visitors were seldom seen. Lurid tales proliferated.

In recent years, a sect of the peacock angel cult from Iraq had taken up quiet occupation of the site, though no one could say when exactly they gathered, or if any reverend or imam had taken up permanent residence in the church. The faithful came and went in ones and twos at odd hours.

When a local child or spinster spoke of hearing the strains of a choir chanting in the deep hours of the night, the account was usually dismissed for having coincided with the noise of a thunderstorm. Surely the place didn't draw sufficient numbers for a choir. There were no signs posted regarding services. The only visible change to the stone facade was an iron emblem: An encircled triangle, nailed to the door. Strangers knocked on that red door, as the short man in the vest did now, rain dripping from his hair. They knocked, and when the door opened, spoke a word into a gap from which no light escaped. And if they were granted entrance, the same observer could never attest to witnessing their exit.

Abdelmalek closed the door behind him. He didn't recognize the woman who had accepted the password, but here, passing through the curtain into the vestibule was a face he knew, a face tattooed with the thorny letters of a language last spoken on the plateau of Leng. The Reverend Ciprian flicked his eyes in Abdelmalek's direction before stepping forward to place his hands on the shoulders of the woman in the burka. There had been no telegrams or letters to announce their arrival. The church had no phone service, and any attempt to forecast the meeting would have been too risky with the eyes and ears of SPEAR upon them. There was only so much their man inside the agency could do to divert that surveillance. So why was there such knowing in the reverend's eyes, even before he lifted the burka from the woman's head. Had he dreamt of this moment?

Cyprian inhaled deeply at the sight of her. "Salome." The name came out choked, laden with suppressed emotion. "The papers…they said you were killed in a raid."

Salome touched the reverend's cheek. A tear had formed in the ink-stained crow's feet at the corner of his eye. She wiped it away with the pad of her thumb. Tentatively, but perhaps emboldened by her touch, he reached out and laid a hand on the black cloth that covered her belly, causing her to flinch and touch his wrist.

"The baby," he said. "I'm so sorry."

Salome shook her head. "The baby is fine. I'm just tender from powder burns."

"We apologize for any distress you've suffered," Abdelmalek said. "It was necessary that the papers carried news of her death. Thanks to brother Jeremy's brave efforts, both SPEAR and the Golden Bough believe the child died with the mother."

"How can this be?"

"Reverend, forgive me, but it's been a long trip. We passed through the city on our way here, to secure the amulet." Abdelmalek patted his vest pocket and Ciprian's eyes widened. The news that the jewel was secure would take some of the edge off of what he had to explain next. "May we come in? I imagine Salome could use some refreshment. It was a hot day for hiding under a veil."

"Yes, of course, please. Would you like some sweet tea?"

"Thank you," Salome said. "That would be lovely."

Cyprian held the red velvet curtain aside and waved the two of them into the nave. They followed him to an aisle between the rows of pews, then down a winding stair to a kitchen in the basement, where the woman who had answered Abdelmalek's knock set about preparing the tea. Abdelmalek thought she was probably younger than she looked dressed in the traditional garb. A single skunk stripe of white ran from her temple to a braided bun. A silver sigil hung from a chain around her neck.

The reverend offered them chairs and assisted Salome as she settled into hers. The woman set a plate of figs, cheese, and bread on the dark wood table and lit candles before withdrawing to a place in the shadows beside an ancient, grease-stained stove where a kettle rattled above a blue flame.

Ciprian waited for Abdelmalek to speak, legs crossed beneath his robes, fingers laced around his knee.

Abdelmalek cleared his throat. "Jack Parsons, the rocket scientist I told you about, has made great progress toward a medium of manifestation. So much that we have him to thank for the conception."

The reverend looked pained at this but kept his silence.

"Our most recent experiment resulted in the near physical emergence of Azothoth."

"Near?"

"The powder isn't perfect, but it's close enough to bring the god into a sphere that touches both worlds."

Ciprian looked at Salome. "I imagine Salome's voice deserves more credit for that success than you're willing to confess."

"No, Reverend. With all due respect for her gifts, we've reached a limit. Salome's voice has been fixed since she reached womanhood. A voice alone won't provide a breakthrough until her child matures. Jack, however, could achieve a breakthrough with his smoke which transcends that limit."

Ciprian passed the platter of food to Salome. She politely selected a fig and ate while he asked, "How is it that you and the baby survived this...*experiment,* my dear?" And turning a hard gaze on Abdelmalek, "And why in the name of R'lyeh would you risk their wellbeing with a rite doomed to failure?"

Abdelmalek straightened his spine. "We accomplished two things, reverend. We verified that Jack's smoke can embody the harmonic event to a degree undreamt of before—"

"Don't try to bedazzle me with jargon! You have no patience, Kamen. If it takes a generation, then so be it. We don't need to bring in outsiders. We've waited eons already."

"*And*...we convinced the government and a rival order that the voice died with Salome. You have Parsons to thank for that, too. He and brother Jeremy staged a brilliant piece of theater in the desert. And Salome played her part like a Hollywood starlet."

Salome rubbed her belly unconsciously. When the gesture drew the reverend's eye, she took a sip of tea. "He's an expert with explosives," she said. "He placed a pair of small charges in my clothes with a bag of chicken blood."

"Fake gunshots," Abdelmalek interjected. "Jack bought us time. A generation, if we *need* it, but I don't believe we will. All his life, he's been laboring to bring mankind to the stars, but now he will bring the lords of the stars to us."

"I wish you could have seen it," Salome said to Ciprian. "It was beautiful. And so close."

"And you trust this...*thelemite*?" The question was wholly directed at Salome. "You are the vessel of the prophecy. Tell me what you would have us do, and I will abide by it. Tell me what brings you here."

Salome glanced at the woman by the stove and traced a lazy circle on the scratched table with a fingernail. "We need passage. Anonymous passage. Jeremy got us this far by train, but from here, I would take the old paths north, the subterranean ways. So that I might raise my child among his cousins in Massachusetts.

The reverend stroked his beard. "It will be arranged. You will sleep here tonight and I'll prepare a boat in the morning. Will you accompany her, Kamen?"

"No. I need to leave the country. My work with Parsons is done for now. Our adversaries believe we've failed, but there are still artifacts that threaten our future. The scarab, dagger, and mirror. I will scatter them far from the shores where Salome will raise our greatest hope."

The reverend laced his fingers into the mudra of the dark star. "So mote it be."

June 18, 1952

Case # 156418

Field Report: Pasadena, CA

Subject: Death of John Whiteside Parsons (age 37)

Investigation of the explosion at 1071 South Orange Grove

Due to our ongoing surveillance of the subject, Agent Whittaker and I arrived at the scene before local police and firefighters. Examination of the debris revealed fragments of occult writings and chemical formulas consistent with our theory of the case, namely that Parsons was still actively engaged in testing new iterations of his trans-dimensional manifestation medium.

Brief interviews with Parsons' neighbors, Ganci and Fosshaug, turned up no useful details. Marjorie Cameron Parsons was unavailable for comment.

The coach house where the accident occurred was well stocked with volatile chemicals, including nitroglycerin, trinitrobenzene, and penthaerythritol tetra nitrate. The local authorities will likely attribute the blast to improper handling of fulminate of mercury, which Parsons is believed to have been working with at the time. It is surmised that he was mixing the volatile chemical in a coffee can and dropped it, setting off a chain reaction with his other explosive stores.

While there are indeed similarities to the flattening of structures by invisible force documented in the Dunwich case of 1928, it is my initial finding that this is mere coincidence. I found no conclusive evidence that Parsons attained his long sought breakthrough with a compound of sufficient efficacy to cause a trans-dimensional event without the aid of a genetically gifted vocalist.

Nevertheless, Agent Whittaker and I confiscated all traces of the arcane smoke powders before the remaining chemicals were removed from the site by the 58th Ordnance Disposal Unit of the US Army.

These samples were logged at the new secure SPECTRA facility at the China Lake Naval Station shortly before midnight on June 17th, 1952.

Yours,

Jeremy LeBlanc

Agent Jeremy Leblanc

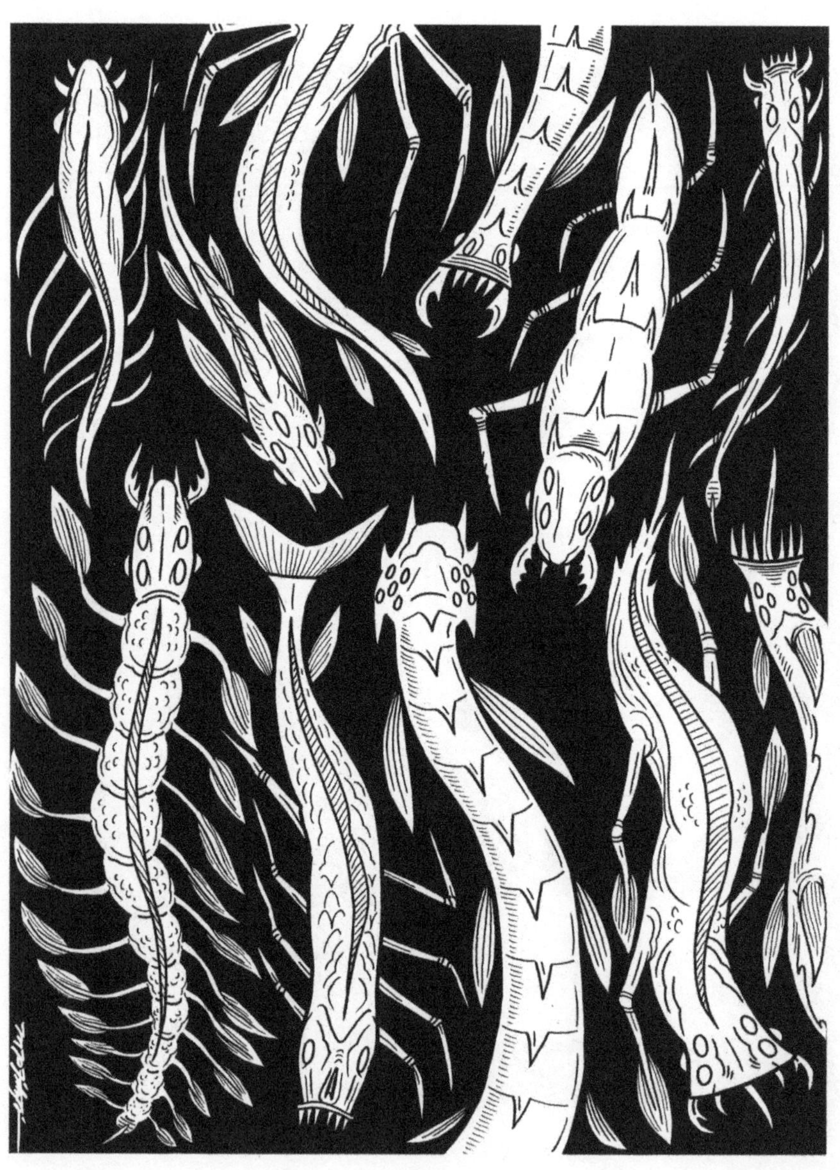

Acknowledgements

Smoke & Dagger had its genesis when Mat Fitzsimmons, a reader of the SPECTRA books, sent me some artwork inspired by my additions to the Cthulhu Mythos. One thing led to another, the stack of drawings grew, and somewhere along the line Mat suggested that I should write a story about Jack Parsons, the pioneering rocket engineer and occultist who blew himself up in 1952 and has a crater on the dark side of the moon named for him (cue the Pink Floyd soundtrack). It wasn't the first time a reader had suggested I do something with Parsons, so I figured I should take the hint.

Given Jack's fascination with the occult, his involvement with classified government projects, and the false accusations of espionage that briefly cost him his security clearance, he and his milieu did seem tailor-made for a SPECTRA Files adventure. Once I did the math and realized that he could have crossed paths with Becca Philips' grandmother Catherine when she was Becca's age, the urge to blend fact and fiction became irresistible.

Like any historical fiction, the book you now hold in your hands called for a good bit of research. I owe a primary debt to George Pendle's excellent biography of Parsons, *Strange Angel*. The CBS TV series based on Pendle's book does a great job of capturing the atmosphere of the era and the essential passion of Jack Parsons, but in some ways it's as fictionalized as my novella. I urge anyone interested in the real John Whiteside Parsons to pick up Pendle's biography. If you do, you'll discover that though my aim was to blur the lines of fact and fiction around Parsons, some of the weirdest stuff about him is what's true.

For the details of Catherine's 1940s New York stomping grounds, I found great helpers in the research librarians who haunt those halls today. Mai Reitmeyer at the American Museum of Natural History sent me scans of the 1949 exhibit halls guidebook, while Martha Tenney and Shannon O'Neill at the Barnard Archives furnished the same for the college's Anthropology course catalogue of that year. The Metropolitan Museum's publication, *The New York Obelisk: How Cleopatra's Needle Came to New York and What Happened When it Got Here* by Martina D'Alton provided a treasure trove of cool details to spark my imagination, and if you go looking for info on the freemasons who brought the obelisk to America, you'll find the one instance where I combined two historical figures into a single fictional character.

I owe my greatest thanks on this project to my collaborator, Mat Fitzsimmons, for his stunning art, clever cyphers, and generous spirit. Next up, my writer friend Nick Nafpliotis provided valuable creative support, editorial guidance, and the perfect title. Chuck Killorin, an early reader of all the SPECTRA books (and cover artist for the trilogy) read a rough draft and gave me the confidence to see it through, while Matthew Bright captured the feel of this prequel episode with a cover that sings. Robert S. Wilson polished the final edit on a tight deadline, and Jill Sweeney-Bosa was kind enough to lend her sharp eye and red pen to proofreading under pressure. Any errors of fact or grammar that slipped through are mine.

Love to Jen and River, who keep my life happy, stable, and creative. And special thanks to you, faithful reader of my weird tales. Without your support this story would never have been told.

DOUGLAS WYNNE wrote his first novel in high school but took a creative detour to spend the next decade writing songs and singing in rock bands before coming full circle back to fiction. He is the author of *The Devil of Echo Lake, Steel Breeze,* and the SPECTRA Files trilogy (*Red Equinox, Black January,* and *Cthulhu Blues*). His most recent short stories have appeared in the anthologies *I Am The Abyss* and *A Secret Guide to Fighting Elder Gods*. He lives in Massachusetts with his wife and son and a houseful of animals.

Artist/musician MAT FITZSIMMONS has contributed graphics to the underground (music posters; surf, skate, snowboard art; punk 'zines; independent books) for over 25 years, along with fronting the savage rock juggernaut, Herbert/Automatic Animal (1993-2018). A life-long resident, Fitz lives in Santa Cruz, CA with wife Brandi and giant cat Chloe, where he draws inspiration from the shadows of the mountains to the depths of the sea. Contact: feralteethpress@gmail.com

THE
SPECTRA
FILES
ANCIENT EVIL
MODERN TECH
FAMILY SECRETS
GOVERNMENT LIES
RED EQUINOX
1
DOUGLAS WYNNE
BLACK JANUARY
A SPECTRA FILES NOVEL
2
DOUGLAS WYNNE
CTHULHU BLUES
3
DOUGLAS WYNNE
THE SAGA CONTINUES

CPSIA information can be obtained
at www.ICGtesting.com
Printed in the USA
LVHW090108071219
639737LV00003B/444/P

9 781077 266834